I0459591

Merry with My Family

Merry with My Family

A CHRISTMAS COMEDY

—

Shelton Johnson

Part II of the Family Comedy Trilogy

Copyright © 2016 Shelton Johnson
All rights reserved. Including the right of reproduction in whole or in part in
any form.
Cover Illustration and Design provided by Ms. Camile Maddow
ISBN-13: 9780692778685
ISBN-10: 0692778683

Dedicated to my parents and grandparents, who
have shown unconditional love for one another
in over eighty years of marriage combined

Table of Contents

CHAPTER 1

In the Air

I was pissed off. I couldn't get any sleep in this noisy airport. To make matters worse, my fifteen-year-old daughter, Angel, and her boyfriend, Javier, sat on the other side of the back-to-back seating where I laid. Javier was the artsy type, with curly hair, a five o'clock shadow, and a skin tone that could pass for any race. He seemed like a good kid. I just couldn't relate to him, all he talked about was his art.

I had my eyes shut tighter than a pepper-sprayed Chinese man. I was trying my best to fall back asleep when I overheard their whispering conversation. Angel asked curiously, "Have you?"

"No, have you?" Javier answered.

"No, do you want to right now?" Angel responded.

Javier sounded scared, which I was happy about. "Are you serious? Right here? Right now? We're in an airport, and your dad is right there."

"Don't worry about him," Angel said. "That's just my stepdad."

I popped up, startling not only them but also my wife, Tiffany, who sat two seats down from me. Tiffany asked what was wrong with me. I ignored her as I looked back at them with my face tight and my eyes piercing with anger. They looked at me, frightened with big eyes, before Angel spoke up to say that they were talking about kissing. I glanced at Tiffany from the corner of my eye while smacking my lips to mumble, "Kissing my ass."

I noticed the tremendous amount of sunlight bursting through the oversized airport windows, reflecting off the ornaments that hung on the fake tree next to our terminal. In my peripheral vision, I saw Uncle Al standing at the terminal, not in line, waving us toward him.

Uncle Al had a new part-time job as an aircraft mechanic for Southwest Airlines. All he really did was change the brakes on the tires. The good part was, since it was an airplane, he couldn't test-drive it. He flew up to BWI from South Carolina to get us free flights to Los Angeles using his employee advantage so that we could spend Christmas with Tiffany's family.

As I grabbed my luggage off the stiff, blue airport chairs, I told Angel and Tiffany to do the same so that we could begin boarding. I saw Tiffany and Angel look at each other, as if something were going on. I asked Tiffany, "What is it?"

"Well, Angel wanted me to ask one last time," she said. "Is there any way your Uncle Al could find a seat on the plane for Javier?"

I looked back at her, then at Javier, and finally at Angel when I said, "No, Angel. You should be happy that you're going. If we weren't flying Southwest, you would be a baggage fee short."

Uncle Al was losing patience as I noticed Javier walking toward me, speaking with his natural Italian accent. It sounded like something you would hear in a low-budget romantic film. "I completely understand and respect your decision Mr. Stuart. One day, when I am a man, I too will be forced to make difficult decisions."

I said, "Well, it really wasn't difficult at all, but thank you." Tiffany nudged me on the arm, and I saw Angel roll her eyes and shake her head before I asked, "So Javier, what *do* you plan on doing when you are a man?"

He answered, "No Mr. Stuart, I do not have a plan. I will live an inspired lifestyle, as I do now. When I am moved by something, or when I feel something, I run to my canvas, grab my brush, and paint until my vision is within my grasp."

I was thinking to myself: *I must've been inspired earlier when I ran into the airport bathroom and grabbed that bar in the handicap stall.* I didn't have a vision, but I definitely had some victims, who walked in after me.

Angel was looking at Javier all googly-eyed because of his answer to my question. Tiffany and I looked at each other in disbelief. We knew everything Javier had said just equals out to unemployment. He then asked me, "What inspires you Mr. Stuart?"

Playfully, I imitated his accent as I answered, "Ah, Mr. Javier, I seem to be inspired by bills."

"I did not know you were a Buffalo Bills fan Mr. Stuart," Javier commented.

"Ah, that's because I am not, Mr. Javier. I am a fan of the electric bills, water bills, insurance bills." Tiffany nudged me to stop.

That took the smile right off Javier's face. Angel was in shock, and Tiffany shook her head in evident disapproval of my immature actions. Tiffany told Angel and Javier to say their good-byes, so we could leave. Their hug was so long and drawn out. I've seen less drama in Lifetime movies.

It was nearing noon on December 24, 2015, when we boarded the plane. I was in the window seat, and Tiffany sat in the middle beside me, while Angel sat near the aisle. Uncle Al sat in the seat directly behind me, next to a heavy-chested woman. When the stewardess came by asking who wanted refreshments, Uncle Al would use his left arm to grab some. He only did that so he could feel her breasts. I had never seen anyone consume that much peanuts and water.

I couldn't focus on my uncle's cheap thrills though; I had issues of my own I was dealing with. Once the plane took off, I began to feel turbulence pressure on my stomach. I immediately regretted that breakfast burrito from Taco Bell I ate at the airport. Angel was still upset and pouting about having to leave Javier. This was made clear by her leaning back in her chair with her arms crossed tightly across her chest. She looked straight ahead, as if seeing her mom and me would make her catch a deadly disease. Angel's attitude came to an end though, when she received a text from presumably Javier. However, all cell phones were supposed to be off during this point of the flight. The volume of her ring tone drew the attention of the other passengers. I could tell that Tiffany was embarrassed as Angel texted back, smiling. Tiffany whispered to me, "Stu, can you believe this?" I put my hand up, asking her to stop talking to me. All I could think about was Taco Bell, tequila, lowriders, and anything else Mexican because of the way my stomach felt.

Tiffany shook her head in frustration toward me before turning to face Angel. "Get off that phone. You are embarrassing us, and you know it isn't supposed to be on right now."

Angel didn't even look up from texting to argue with her mom, claiming that one phone won't take a plane down. Tiffany quickly snatched the phone out of Angel's hand, threw it in her purse, and zipped the purse closed. Angel tried to reach for it, but that was stopped by a hard slap to the hand from Tiffany. Angel jolted herself back in her seat, crossing her arms and looking forward again while mumbling, "Y'all don't ever let me have any fun."

Over the past few years, Angel had physically developed into a young lady. She'd also developed a need to be cute at all times. Angel used to never care about hair, nails, and shoes. Now, she wouldn't even leave the house without all three being stylish. Even though she was going through that teenage stage of thinking her mom and I were "so not cool," I still loved her and would do just about anything for her.

The turbulence had finally ended, and I was still trying to get myself together. Tiffany was quietly reading a book, while Uncle Al was knocked out, snoring, and drooling on the airplane window. Angel had her headphones on as she listened to music from her tablet, which lay on the tray connected to the passenger seat in front of her. Angel used her hands to beat on the tray while rocking along to the songs. Before long, the guy sitting in front of her turned and asked, "Excuse me, I'm trying to get some rest. Could you please stop hitting the tray?"

Angel answered with an attitude. "No, you're not my daddy. This is my tray."

The man then stood up to face Angel, and he was intimidating. Instead of me trying to describe him, just imagine that Kimbo Slice and Precious had a baby. This nice, kindhearted, courteous, friendly (he's watching me write), outstanding example of a gentleman said with a flaring voice, "I know I'm not your dad! If I were, you would be getting a much-needed ass whipping right now."

Tiffany's and Angel's mouths dropped in awe of what he had said. "What! Who do you think you're talking to!" Tiffany yelled before looking at me and asking, "Stu, you're just going to let him stand there and say that to our daughter?"

That mild-mannered, lovable guy became excited about the thought of revenge. "Oh, she's your daughter?!" he questioned while pointing in my direction.

I've never been prouder to say, "I'm just the stepdaddy." That real man of genius took his seat as Angel continued to listen to her music without banging on the tray. Now, I know I said earlier that I would do just about anything for Angel, but you can go ahead and put this situation in the "just about" category.

A few hours passed before I woke up from my nap to find Angel asleep and Tiffany playing a game on her phone, which was unusual because she usually reads or listens to music. "You OK?" I asked.

Tiffany rolled her eyes. "Oh, you're concerned now? Where was all that concern at earlier, when that big lima bean–eating bastard was yelling at Angel?" I was getting ready to explain when Tiffany put her hand up and shook her head with her eyes closed. "It's OK. I really don't want to hear it Stu. It'll only make me more upset." I blew out hard as I sank into my seat and gazed at the clouds through my window. To my surprise, Tiffany began to speak: "It's not just you Stu. I'm hoping that my parents can at least be cordial this weekend. You know, with Angel being there and all."

I said I understood before turning to see Tiffany facing straight ahead. "Besides, she's a teenager now," I continued. "She's probably heard worse at her high school."

Tiffany rolled her eyes in my direction before saying, "You clearly have never heard my parents argue."

Tiffany was nervous about her parents being cordial because they'd been divorced for nearly five years. I couldn't remember the reason why, so I asked her to remind me. She said, "Remember when we flew over there to see them on Christmas Day back in 2010 and my mom was talking about starting her own business?"

"Yeah."

Tiffany went on to say, "Well, she opened it up. Nancy's Fish Fry and Yoga Studio. Unbeknown to my dad though, she had taken a huge chunk out of their savings to get it started. So if you ask my dad, he says that joint accounts caused the divorce. If you ask my mom, she says my dad's mouth caused the divorce, because ever since he found out, he has been rude and disrespectful toward her."

"How did Frank not know that a chunk of their savings was missing?" I asked.

"Well, not everybody is cheap enough to check their bank accounts three times a day like you Stu." I smacked my lips while briefly turning away from her, before she continued. "Just playing Stu. Seriously though, my dad *hates* technology. He made a ton of money in the eighties and nineties, making and selling how-to videos on VHS. That's how we were able to move from Inglewood to Santa Monica, California. As you know though, everything now is on YouTube, which he hates more than anything, and is the reason why my parents don't have smartphones."

"So your dad is pretty good at fixing stuff?" I asked.

Tiffany answered, "Yeah, when we were little, we had a dog named Tricky Trap." After Tiffany saw my face pull back, she took the time to explain. "No, see, he was a rescued dog that was found in a raccoon trap. So naturally, when we heard his story, we decided to name him Trap. Then, after about a week or so, we noticed that he couldn't close his mouth on one side. So we started calling him Tricky Trap. I think the problem had something to do with his jaw."

I curiously asked, "How did y'all find out about it?"

Tiffany shrugged her shoulders. "Well, we kept noticing his food all over the floor, and him barking at his bowl. So for years, we would push all his food to the left side of the bowl to make it easier for him to eat. Until one day, after going for a walk, he was excited to eat. Tricky Trap ran to his bowl and knocked it over. His Kibbles 'n Bits were all over the kitchen floor. My dad saw him struggling and helped him by turning his head to the left every time he bent over for food. It looked like my daddy was baptizing Tricky Trap on the kitchen floor. That night, my dad used some scrap parts in the shed to build him a neck brace to wear when he was eating. It worked great too."

I nodded. "Yeah, anytime somebody can build a neck brace for a dog using spare parts, they're pretty handy."

Tiffany quickly commented, "Don't mention the dog around my sister Teresa though. She still holds his death against me."

I faced my palms up, signaling, "Why?"

"Me and Tricky Trap were in the woods playing when I saw a bee's nest hanging from a tree. It looked old because I didn't see any bees flying near it. So while he barked at it, I hit it with a stick to knock it down because I wanted to see what it looked like on the inside. A bunch of bees came out, and I took off running. Tricky Trap stood there, barking at them. Since his coat was so thick, they really couldn't sting his body good. That's when I noticed the bees, just flying in and out of his mouth. I started screaming, 'Run Trap! Run!' It was too late though. By the time I came back with my dad, all the bees were gone, and Tricky Trap was lying there dead."

I sympathized, "I'm sorry to hear that Tiff. That's a rough way for your pet to die."

"Yeah, my dad felt the same way too. That's why he built a box for him to be buried in. We ended up having a nice little funeral for Tricky Trap in the backyard too."

"Oh, well that's good," I said.

Tiffany nodded. "Yeah, it was an opened-mouth/closed-casket funeral."

I couldn't help but laugh. Still trying to get her to relax about the visit, I told her, "Look at the bright side. They found a way to get back together again."

"They're not back together again. My mom just moved back because her business failed."

I cut her off. "I could've told you that was gonna happen."

"I thought it was a great business idea. Downtown Santa Monica needs a one-stop shop for fried fish and yoga."

I looked at Tiffany like she was crazy, right before I asked, "So why are we going over there?"

"Well, this is the first Christmas my parents have been in the same house together since their divorce back in 2011. I'm hoping that we can recreate that same feeling we used to have on Christmas Day with everyone being there. Plus, I didn't want to go visit while they weren't living together. I don't want to see them that way."

"So what was Christmas like for you growing up?" I inquired.

She paused as the smile on her face grew to its full potential. "Magical, just magical. My mom would always wait until Christmas Eve night to decorate the tree, so that when we came downstairs that would be our first time seeing everything together. She would always make it look so pretty, and we couldn't touch a gift until we had taken at least five pictures in front of it. Then, my dad would always wear his Santa Claus hat while he cooked us a huge breakfast with Belgian waffles. My mom banned him from buying gifts though, because he was the worst when it came to that. My sister and I always thought he was so bad at buying gifts because he grew up as an only child. Either way, what he would usually do was give us cash. My mom was the one who made sure we had plenty of gifts to open." Tiffany's voice amplified to say, "Now, at Christmas dinner, that's when my mom threw down. She would make the best meals, and everything was organic too."

I gently placed my arm around Tiffany. "I can understand why you would miss that. I hope you're able to experience that feeling again too."

Eventually, Tiffany got up to use the restroom while I was leaning against the window, gazing at the sky. I could hear Uncle Al texting behind me, so I turned around to whisper, "Hey Unc, thanks for these tickets. It really means a lot to Tiffany for us to be able to visit her family."

"No problem Stu," he said. "I knew when you called me that had I not gotten them, your cheap ass would still be sitting in Maryland. But you're welcome." Trying not to disturb the other passengers, I laughed softly while nodding in agreement with him.

In the past year or so, Uncle Al's appearance had changed a bit. He had lost a little weight from being on that unemployed diet for so long. He now had a few gray hairs sprinkled in his mustache, and he finally got rid of the Jheri Curl and went bald. Thank God. A couple of things hadn't changed though. He still wore his Scorpio medallion, drowned himself in cheap cologne, and smoked Black and Milds.

Still looking back at him texting, I asked, "How did you get Aunt Tammy to let you go on this trip and miss Christmas with her husband? She doesn't even like Tiffany."

Uncle Al brushed me off. "Shiiid, that was easy. I lied and told her I had an interview for a full-time job over here. She packed my bags for me."

I watched Uncle Al smile as he tried to keep up with the texts that were blowing up his phone. Curiously, I questioned, "Who is that Unc?"

Uncle Al looked up at me with his head tilted, bottom lip hanging, and one eyebrow raised before saying, "Is you Tammy? 'Cause if not, don't worry 'bout who I'm texting. I'm a grown-ass man."

"OK, my bad Unc. I didn't know you took texting so seriously." He continued to look at me sideways, now with his eyes bulging, which suggested that I face forward and leave him alone. I turned back around in my seat and saw Tiffany sliding in front of Angel to take her seat. This was immediately followed by the pilot on the loudspeaker saying, "Please prepare for landing!"

—

It was 3:00 p.m. Pacific Time. I stood in line at the rental car desk while Tiffany, Uncle Al, and Angel sat in the waiting area. Fortunately, there was only one person in front of me in line. The company had two people working the desk, each on his own individual computer. It was clear who was the supervisor and who was the employee. The supervisor was finishing with customers a lot faster than his employee, and he had to keep going over there to tell the employee to put on his glasses. He had already quoted a customer the wrong price earlier.

It was just my luck that I got the employee, a tall, thin guy with low-cut hair who could easily pass for a high school basketball player. "Hi, I'm Stuart Jones. I had a reservation for a full-sized sedan," I said.

With his glasses still off, he replied, "Hi Mr. Jones." He began to squint his eyes. "Yes, I see you here. I'm sorry to inform you that the only full-sized vehicle we have left is a 2014 Chevy Impala. It's a fluorescent brown and, to be honest, really quite hideous. Around the office, we call it the Brown Bummer."

"What? Why?"

"Well, you know how Joe Louis was the Brown Bomber, and people cheered for him," he answered. "It's the opposite for this car. When people see it, they are usually disappointed and bummed out."

I remembered how bad his eyesight was and asked if he could call his supervisor over. His supervisor stepped away from his customer to take a look. "Ah, yes sir, the Brown Bummer," he said. The middle-aged foreigner with an Iranian accent continued, "Sir, this is our most returned vehicle. Claude will see if we can do anything to help you."

He walked away, and Claude the employee offered, "Mr. Jones, we can upgrade you to an SUV for only twenty dollars more. I'm sorry, but we can't make it a free upgrade since we technically still have a full-sized sedan available. But again, I wouldn't drive it."

I was thinking to myself: *I know you wouldn't. You couldn't drive a hard bargain with your blind ass.* I simply said, "No, I won't do the upgrade. I'll just take the Impala. I'm only here for two days. That's not worth twenty dollars."

The car was tawny brown; its fluorescent-style paint job, underneath the garage lights, made it stand out from the rest. Really, I'm just using a bunch of words to tell you that it looked like a shiny piece of shit. Like all the customers before me, I too was bummed. Tiffany and Angel didn't say anything when they saw it, even though their facial expressions displayed evident disappoint- ment. When Uncle Al saw it, he blew up. "Aw HELL NAW Stu! HELL NAW!" As the four of us stood in the nearly empty garage, about ten yards away from the Impala, I told him what happened at the register, and he got even more pissed, "WHAT! A blind man said he wouldn't drive it, and you still went with it?! For twenty dollars?!"

"Uncle Al, I've been knowing you all my life," I said. "I've never seen a car that you didn't want to test-drive."

Uncle Al blurted, "Well, you found one today. I wouldn't test-drive this. I'll test-crash it into a tree or test-drown it off a bridge maybe."

Uncle Al was sitting in the back seat next to Angel when he said, "Drop me off at the back of the hotel too. I don't want my first appearance to be in the back seat of a shiny piece of shit."

"Didn't you want to see Frank and Nancy before I took you to the hotel?"

Uncle Al looked up from texting with a smile. "Oh yeah, let me holla at Frank. I haven't seen him since y'all's wedding."

As I drove, my phone began to ring. We hadn't figured out how to use the Bluetooth in the rental car yet, so I put the phone to my ear nervously while looking around for the police. It was my mom calling to tell me Merry Christmas and how much she wished I could be there for the Christmas Eve party they were having that night at their house. After telling her that I wish I could be there too, she began to fill me in on the latest gossip in the family. "You know, BenDaria is coming tonight."

"Oh yeah, how is she doing?" I asked.

My mom responded, "Oh, she doing good. She just bought a house for her and her daughter. She had been saving up all her alimony, child support, and checks from her job as a dental assistant for a while now."

"That's good," I said.

My mom commented, "Yeah, but she still bitter about Jamaal. She won't even let her daughter call Santa Claus Saint Nick."

I laughed a little before asking, "So what's going on with Jamaal? Has anybody heard anything from him lately?"

"BenDaria said after Jamaal got stationed in Florida, Nick started talking to somebody else here in South Carolina. Apparently, Jamaal wants to get back with BenDaria, but she don't want nothing to do with him no more."

I nodded while thinking to myself: *I know what it's like to not be able to keep a woman. So it has to be a pretty shitty feeling to not be able to keep a woman or a man.*

She continued, "Other than that, ain't nothing else going on besides your daddy still getting on my nerves."

I started to grin. "Oh Lord, what he do now?"

"You know Shane helps us put up the Christmas tree every year because your dad's too old to be doing it by himself."

"Yeah," I said.

My mom resumed, "Well, this year, he says he don't feel like doing it. I swear that boy gets lazier by the minute. So your dad went and bought one of those Christmas trees that hang from the rearview mirror and hung it in the kitchen doorway like it was a mistletoe."

"What?" I questioned in disbelief.

She finished by saying, "Yeah. Now all these gifts for the grand-kids, piled up between the living room and the kitchen. If I want to make a sandwich, now I got to walk all the way around and through the dining room. What kind of sense does that make?"

I couldn't respond because of my uncontainable laughter. We finally ended up getting off the phone as we approached Tiffany's parents' house.

CHAPTER 2

Greetings

We turned into the cul-de-sac, and Tiffany's parents' house was straight ahead. They lived in a light gray colonial-style home, with blue shutters, that showcased an oversized two-car garage. The brick-paved driveway extended throughout the walkway, which led to a concrete stoop. I rang the doorbell as we stood there staring at the wooden door that was painted to match the shutters. Before the door opened, I could clearly hear Tiffany's dad scream, "Oh, you'll tell me somebody's at the door, but yo' ass won't go get it?"

This was immediately followed by the door being yanked open by Tiffany's dad. After greeting him, I walked in. As I stood there listening to Uncle Al and Frank catch up on old times, I noticed the five-by-seven framed photo of Tricky Trap on the end of the table. He was wearing his wooden brace.

The house was just as gorgeous on the inside as it was on the outside. All the common areas were covered with wood flooring. When you first walked in, you were standing in the back of the living room. To your right were two dark-brown leather recliners. Each one had a matching full-size sofa alongside it, which led to a large TV mounted above the stonework mantle and gas fireplace.

Looking straight ahead from the front door was an updated kitchen with a bar. To the left of the kitchen was a more formal dining area, which was occupied by a six-seater dining set. Farther left, behind the stairway, was a hallway with three doors on the right and one on the left. The one on the left led to the garage. The first on the right was the laundry room. The second was a full-size bathroom, and the third was a bedroom. To the right of the kitchen was a sliding-glass door, which led to a freshly stained back deck and a spacious, well-groomed backyard that backed into the woods without a fence. To the right of the glass door was another door, which was a bedroom with its own interior bathroom.

To the immediate left of the front door was a stairway that led to a loft-style hallway overlooking the living room beneath the massive vaulted ceiling and extended ceiling fans. There were three doors along the hallway, all of which were bedrooms. The first two bedrooms shared a Jack-and-Jill bathroom. The third room in the hallway, which had a Christmas wreath on its door, had its own internal bathroom.

Still standing in the living room, Uncle Al asked, "Hey Frank, Sabrina told me my boy's out now, and he wanted to swing by to see me and the rest of the family. Do you mind?"

"He ain't no boy, he grown," Frank said. "I don't mind though. Tell him to come by between six and seven. I gotta prep for Klepto."

I was looking forward to meeting my cousin for the first time, and Tiffany said she was excited to see him again too, before Uncle Al asked, "What you call him?"

Frank looked at Uncle Al with half-open eyelids before saying, "Klepto. Klepto Chris is what I call him. That boy will steal anything and will keep everything, except a job."

I thought to myself, *The apple doesn't fall too far from the tree.* Uncle Al laughed off Frank's comment, saying that he would let Chris know what time to come.

Frank was an average-sized guy at six feet tall and two hundred pounds. He didn't have a muscle in sight, but he always dressed like he was about to go compete in a sport. He wore track pants, socks with Under Armour slippers, and a loose-fitting Nike Dri-Fit, which covered his protruding stomach. His skin was dark, with low-cut hair and a thinly trimmed mustache. He looked toward the sliding-glass door with his naturally large, bulging eyes. "This is my daughter, Teresa."

Before Frank could even finish his sentence, Tiffany ran over to greet her sister. It was evident that the feeling of excitement was mutual.

This was my first time meeting her sister in person, since she hadn't been able to make it to our wedding. Now meeting her in person though, I could see why my brother, Shane, was crazy about her. She had the face of a model and wore a sundress that showed off her curvy, wide hips and narrow shoulders. She was built like a Christmas tree. Her perfection of beauty ended for me though, when she smiled. Her teeth were separated like country housing. It looked like she could've flossed with an extension cord. She reached out her hand and said, "Hi Stuart, I'm Teresa, Tiffany's younger sister." Since her teeth were so spread apart, there was a lot of extra wind between her words when she spoke. I started looking around to see if somebody had cut the air on in the house.

I shook her hand. "It's nice to finally meet you."

Teresa nodded with sarcasm. "Yeah, you got the 'finally' part right. Thanks for not holding my sister and my niece hostage this year."

I chuckled. "Yeah, I know it's been a while since we've come to visit. It just wasn't in the budget at the time."

Tiffany jokingly chimed in, "Yes Stu, and we all know how you are with your budget." Everyone laughed, including me. I don't deny my cheapness.

Teresa smacked her lips. "Em. Budget or no budget, girl I wouldn't have no man keeping me from seeing my family. I come and go as I please. Tiff, you better tell that man to know his role. You run that house." The smile left my face immediately, and Tiffany just shook her head to ignore her.

I was just about to tell her off when Frank spoke up. "And speaking of men, this is Teresa's freak, I mean friend, Brittany." A step behind Teresa, off to the right, stood Brittany, a six-foot-tall blond woman with short hair and broad shoulders, appearing to be in the same age bracket as Teresa.

"Friend!" Teresa confirmed as she looked at her dad, who rolled his eyes and turned his head away.

Frank then smirked at Brittany. "Brittany, you know I'm just playing. Thanks again for bringing that oak-wood dresser upstairs for me earlier. I sure do appreciate it."

Brittany shrugged her shoulders to say, "No problem. Anytime Mr. Frank."

If the awkward introduction wasn't enough, Brittany's appearance led me to believe that there was more to her relationship with Teresa. Brittany had tobacco dipped in her bottom lip while greeting us in hiking boots, comfortable-fitting carpenter jeans, and a white V-neck T-shirt. Through the T-shirt, I could see that she was wearing a sports bra. I think it was the industrial-strength model too, because it made her chest look harder than cheap liquor. Either way, I greeted her just the same, as did Uncle Al.

After a brief, lighthearted conversation, Tiffany raised the question, "Where's Mom?"

Frank looked over at Tiffany, lazily pointing up toward the loft. "She's in her room, scared."

"Scared of what?" Tiffany abruptly asked.

Frank answered, "I guess I should tell y'all now. We've been having a little mouse problem this week." Teresa, Tiffany, and Angel gasped for air. Brittany grinned. Frank continued, "Last week, I was in here watching TV when I saw a mouse sitting on the couch, watching TV with food in his hands like he pays rent around here. After I told your mama, she been locking herself in her room ever since."

"Why do you keep saying her room?" Tiffany asked. "Do you guys not sleep together anymore?"

Proudly, Frank answered, "No, we're divorced. Just living together. Matter of fact, I'm hoping she can move out soon." Tiffany shook her head as if she were mentally deleting all of her dad's comments. She then ran upstairs to see her mom, with Angel following close behind.

Teresa and Brittany had already taken seats on the couch in the living room when Tiffany reached the top of the stairs asking, "Which room is hers?"

Frank shouted up, "The one with the ugly paper plate wreath on it that your mama made. Be careful not to open the door too fast, 'cause that cheap shit will fly right off." Frank then looked over at Uncle Al and me. "It's almost four thirty, I need to go pick my dad up from the doctor." I told Frank I would take him, and Uncle Al said that he wanted to come as well.

Once outside, I began to walk toward my rental car. As soon as Frank saw it, he shouted, "I'm not riding in that shiny piece of shit!" Uncle Al was rolling as I smacked my lips. Frank continued, "We can just take my car." Frank then pressed a button to open the garage to his convertible Mercedes. I got a little excited because I had never ridden in a convertible before. When I reached for the door handle, Frank said, "Whoa! Whoa! Whoa! I still need you to drive. I've been drinking." He tossed me the keys.

I looked back at Uncle Al, who is the king of test-driving other people's cars, before he said, "And I'm about to be drinking."

Uncle Al stood beside the minifridge in the garage as he looked at Frank for clearance to grab a beer. Frank said yes and requested that Uncle Al hand him one too.

I was nervous as a cop on camera driving that car. I knew I couldn't afford to fix anything on it. At Uncle Al's request, Frank sat in the back seat with him, making me look like a chauffeur. Uncle Al began to show him the texts on his phone that he wouldn't even talk to me about on the plane, which led to them telling stories and laughing in unison at the times they shared while on double dates with Nancy and her sister Sabrina back in the '80s.

"So what's going on with Brittany, Mr. Frank?" I asked in an attempt to start a conversation that I could be a part of.

He popped his head up from Uncle Al's phone and looked at me with one eyebrow raised. "For what? You interested?"

I quickly responded, "Naw, she's not my type at all. I was just asking, because it was kinda awkward when you introduced her earlier."

Frank and Uncle Al started to laugh. "I know. I'm just messing with you Stu. She works construction full time and moves furniture on the weekends with her pickup truck. She's a nice girl, but her back is too wide for me. She built like a lumberjack. I think it's 'cause she likes to do that CrossFit stuff."

Uncle Al blurted, "Shiiid, it look like she did so much CrossFit, she done crossed genders."

We were supposed to be at the doctor's office by four thirty. Due to my nervously slow driving though, we arrived nearing four forty-five. As I parked the car directly in front of the brick building, alongside the curb, I immediately recognized Frank's dad, George. When he saw us, he began to stand up from the wooden bench seat with black metal railing.

George stood a medium-sized five foot ten with a headful of well-groomed gray hair and matching beard. He wore a gray polo tucked into his creased and cuffed beige khakis, which were held up by a black belt and partially covered his black orthopedic shoes.

As he approached the car, I could hear his loose-fitting watch rattle with every step he took. I had also remembered seeing on Facebook that he had recently become a deacon. "Hey Deacon George!" I said loudly, with intention of an indirect compliment.

George looked at me with his eyes squinted and head pulled back, as if he were trying to read me. He sat in the front passenger seat and then, in complete disregard for my greeting, looked back and rhetorically asked, "Y'all on that CP time ain't you?" Frank apologized for our tardiness before Uncle Al greeted George and reminded him of who he was.

I followed Uncle Al by saying, "And I'm Stuart, your granddaughter Tiffany's husband. You remember? You met me at the wedding."

Frank spoke up. "His memory ain't what it used to be." Frank switched his attention to his father. "Dad, he's the one with all the flowers on Facebook."

George's eyes got big as he snapped his head back in shock. "Oh, that's you?" he asked me with hostility.

"Yes, I like gardening," I said proudly, with a smile.

George responded, "Well I like potato chips, but you don't see me posting pictures of them all over the Internet, do you?" Uncle Al and Frank busted out laughing, as George continued, "Boy, you had me so excited when you sent me that friend request. With all those flowers, I just knew you was a woman trying to check me out. Here it is, you're a man, that likes gardening."

I defended myself by saying, "Well, the name says Stuart on my profile."

George commented while looking away in irritation, "I can't read that little shit!"

I was shocked to hear him curse, which led me to ask, "So I saw you became a deacon?"

He answered with aggravation, "Yeah, why?"

"I was just going to congratulate you."

George was still cranky. "You can save your hot-ass breath on that. I only did it for Sister Patterson. I saw how she was jumping up and down for the pastor. I figured, hell, I got something she can jump up and down on too." Uncle Al, Frank, and I couldn't help but laugh before George continued to speak. "I'm sorry for coming off rude like that. I'm just irritated by this whole deacon thing. I just got a text from the pastor, and he wants me to help hand out Communion on Sunday. I'm telling you, if he keeps bugging me, I might end up getting my stash mixed up with the church stash. Shiiid, pastor think people be sleeping through his sermons now, wait till they get a taste of Hennessey during Communion."

I commented, "Oh, I would've never guessed that from the latest selfie you posted. It was only from the chest up, but it looked like you were wearing a three-piece suit and a top hat. Even the caption said 'Ready for church.'"

After smacking his lips, George shook his head in disagreement. "Naw, I took that on a Wednesday, in the laundry room. Besides, I still had my draws on. I just wanted to update my profile pic."

We all laughed at George's comment as I drove out of the doctor's office parking lot into slow-but-steady traffic. Uncle Al popped his head up from his phone, projecting his voice. "Hold up Stu! You're gonna need to make a left turn at the light."

I squinted my eyes in confusion as I looked at him through the rearview mirror. With quick thought, I realized that he wanted me to take him to whoever he had been texting all day, presumably Sabrina. "No, no, Uncle Al. I'm not taking a married man to another woman's house," I said while still glancing back at him through the rearview mirror.

Uncle Al threw his head back. "Lord have mercy!"

This was followed by Frank saying, "Got damn Stu! I could build a house on your square ass. Let the man go see his baby mama."

George mentioned, "As good as Sabrina looks, you might like what you see. Hell, if I was ten years younger, she would be my baby mama too."

"Come on Stu," Frank explained. "That's the least you could do for your uncle. He flew your whole family out here for free."

Although it was Christmas Eve, the warm California sun reflected off the windshield trim of the convertible. I sat there, gripping the top of the steering wheel with my left hand, as three sets of eyes stared at me like it was my turn to bid in a game of spades. Eventually, when the time came, I granted Uncle Al's request and made the left turn.

We arrived at Sabrina's brick, ranch-style home with a screened-in front porch, in a quiet community in Inglewood. After putting the car in park, I said, "This is a nice house."

As Uncle Al was getting out, he responded by grunting and rolling his eyes. "Hmm, as much as I paid in child support, I thought she'd be living in the Taj Mahal." As Uncle Al rang the doorbell, I noticed three pair of shoes on the stairs leading to the porch.

From the back seat, Frank asked, "Hey, Dad, before I forget, how did the doctor's appointment go?"

George perked up. "It went good. They told me exactly what I wanted to hear."

Frank said, "Good. So did they give you the prescription for the—"

George cut him off with a lifted but scratchy voice. "Hey hey, I don't trust this boy like that, to be telling all my business." Mr. George lowered his voice back to normal tone while adjusting his body in the seat for comfort. "I got my prescription, and I need to go to the drugstore is all."

I couldn't believe it, but Frank vouched for me. "It's OK—he's cool Dad. Just a little awkward sometimes."

"I don't know about that," George said. "Look at how he drives with his left hand. He was leaning toward me." George turned from Frank to look at me before asking rhetorically, "Don't you know you're supposed to drive with your right hand and lean on the window when there is another man in the passenger seat? Come on Stu, be Amsterdamish."

I was hesitant to speak up for myself. "Um, I've never been to Europe before, Mr. George."

George responded with one palm up and his face squished together as he looked at me, appearing to be just as lost as I was. "Well, I've never been to Europe either, but what made you say that?"

I humbly answered, "Um, well you told me to be Amsterdamish. I'm not sure what you mean by that."

"Drive with your right hand instead of your left!" George shouted.

Now irritated, I raised my voice back at him. "Mr. George, you talking about being ambidextrous!"

"Yeah, that's what I said," George said.

I shook my head in frustration before Frank butted in to calm things down. "So other than your prescription, how was everything else?"

"Oh, they told me the usual. High blood pressure, high cholesterol, my back is getting worse, same as my knees, I need to eat healthier, work out more, and drink more water. But the good news is…" He smiled before resuming. "They told me I'm healthy enough for sex." While looking at me, George questioned, "Speaking of sex, when am I going to become a great-grandfather again?"

I rolled my eyes. "Hmm, no time soon with the way Tiffany feels about me right now. She's upset with me about some stuff that happened earlier today."

Mr. George asked, "You had booty on your mind when you got married, didn't you?" He was right, but I didn't want to answer because I could feel Frank looking at me from the back seat. George continued, "No it's fine, you can say it. You probably thought after you said 'I do,' you were going to get all the booty you wanted, whenever you wanted it, right?" I nodded in agreement before George resumed, "I know. I did too, with Frank's mother." Frank rolled his eyes, leaned back in his seat, and began to play on his phone. George said, "I was just like you. My wife and I weren't friends before we got married either. It was strictly lust for me at first, with the beauty of her youth. Then I appreciated her because she supported me and was a great mother to our only child. Once he was old enough to fend for himself though, that's when she became my best friend. In what we used to like to call our 'second wind,' I was able to love her in all three ways. It seems like as soon as we had it all figured out, she was gone."

I spoke with sincerity. "I'm sorry to hear that Mr. George."

He briefly turned away and waved me off. "Don't be sorry for me. I'm thankful I had the opportunity to share my life with her. Lord willing, people get old and die. That's just how it is. But she made getting old fun."

I was sitting there feeling pretty bad because a minute ago, I couldn't stand this old man. Mr. George then said, "So about you and Tiffany's argument now, you need to go back to your wedding day. See, something happens during a wedding that most people completely overlook, forget about, or maybe even just don't care about or know the significance of. That is, when the father gives his daughter's hand in marriage. It's not just him saying he's OK with you marrying his daughter. That conversation should have happened before she had a ring on her finger. When a father passes his daughter's hand to you, he is passing not only the responsibility of taking care of her but also the responsibility to uphold the standard of unconditional love which he has shown her. I don't need to know the details of what you and my granddaughter have going on. I'll just tell you to keep on loving her unconditionally."

"Wow Mr. George, from first impression, I would've never thought you would say something like that," I told him.

"Thanks, I learned a few things over the years. I still try to tell my son Frank, 'cause him and Nancy argue something serious. He don't want to listen to me though."

I concurred. "Yeah, Tiff told me their arguments are ridiculous."

Up until this point, Uncle Al had been waiting for the door to be answered when suddenly, the door swung open, grabbing our attention and cutting Frank off from responding to his father's comments. From the car, we were unable to see the person Uncle Al was speaking with. Eventually, Uncle Al came back to the car, and I began to drive back to Frank's house. Mr. George asked, "What happened? Who was that who answered the door?"

Uncle Al was rapidly texting as he replied, "That was some lil guy saying he was Sabrina's boyfriend. He looked like he could've been a stunt man for Emmanuel Lewis."

Frank questioned, "So she wasn't home?"

Uncle Al said, "Nope, at least that's what her boyfriend said."

While he was still texting I asked, "So who did you say you were?"

Uncle Al looked up briefly before looking back at his phone. "Oh, I just told him I was an old friend of the family. I'm almost fifty-five years old. I don't want no trouble."

George scratched his head. "That still doesn't make any sense though. Why would she tell you to come over if she knew she wasn't going to be there, and even worse, her boyfriend was there?"

Uncle Al replied to his question. "I don't know Mr. George. I'm texting Sabrina now, trying to figure that out. The only thing

I can guess is that maybe she wanted me to come over earlier. Her pocket-sized boyfriend did tell me he had just got home from work."

Frank added, "You know, she runs a day care too. So maybe she had to go take the kids somewhere."

I chuckled while saying, "Well, that explains those little G.I. Joe shoes that were sitting on the stairs." Nobody laughed. I mumbled, "Forget y'all." Soon after, Otis Redding's version of "Merry Christmas Baby" came on the radio, and we all hummed along in enjoyment for the remainder of the ride home.

We pulled into the driveway with the music still playing. Due to the volume, I vaguely heard George ask, "Whose shiny piece of shit is that in the driveway?" Thank goodness I was the only one who heard him.

The time was now six o'clock, and my father-in-law, Frank, had jumped out of the car, neglecting to close the car door behind him as he ran into the house. Concerned with what possibly could be going on, George, Uncle Al, and I followed not too far behind. While locking the door behind me, I overheard Nancy, who stood in the kitchen with Tiffany, say to Frank, "Brittany and Teresa went last-minute shopping, and Angel is upstairs in my room." Frank was running around grabbing everything he could, like a blind man in a whorehouse. After briefly greeting Tiffany with a wave from the foyer, I asked, "What are you doing Frank?"

Clearly fatigued, he didn't even stop for a breather to answer, "The Klepto cleanup. Stu, did you lock all the car doors?" I nodded yes. Uncle Al smacked his lips and shoved his hands down to show disagreement with Frank's comments. Uncle Al couldn't say anything though; Chris's criminal record had proven Frank to be right. Frank finished, "Good, good. Leave your luggage in there too. I swear that boy will steal anything, and get away with it too! I'm telling you, he's about as slippery as deviled eggs."

Uncle Al excused himself to use the restroom before Nancy walked toward me with arms open wide. "Hey Stuart, it's so good to see you again."

We hugged as I agreed, "It's nice to see you again too Ms. Nancy."

With a smile, she said, "You can just call me Ma."

Gleefully I said, "OK, Ma," before looking up at Frank, who had stopped everything he was doing and stood behind the couch, staring at me.

"I'm still Mr. Frank," he said with a straight face and a quick head nod.

Nancy spoke up. "Ignore him. Chris ain't that bad."

Nearly finished locking away everything of value, Frank told Nancy, "You wouldn't know. The only time you come out of your room is to eat, just like you're doing now."

Mr. George, who had stood beside me this entire time, moaned on his way to the couch to watch a western, "Oh boy, here they go."

Tiffany and I sat on the couch across from George to not only join him but also to allow Frank and Nancy to finish their argument.

My mother-in-law, Nancy, looked like a mature version of my wife, with a slightly darker complexion. Her skin was smooth, with the exception of a few moles that had formed around her eyes due to aging. She displayed a full and healthy white smile with a naturally petite physique, which was covered with presentable, house-style clothing.

Suddenly, over the TV's volume, we heard Nancy raise her voice toward Frank: "Get out of my face! You uncircumcised, anteater-dick-having, one-nut-slinging crack baby!"

George cut the TV off to listen as Frank defended himself proudly: "I ain't no damn crack baby!" Since that was the only thing he stood up for, it led me to believe that he was uncircumcised and only had one nut.

George confirmed it though, by asking, "Son, you only have one nut?"

"Look, it's a long story," Frank pleaded.

Nancy butted in with sharp attitude. "No it ain't. We went to buy bikes to get back in shape. The man at the store told Frank he needed to switch the seat out on the bike. The previous owner had a woman's seat on it." Nancy began to imitate Frank's voice. "Frank said, 'Naw, naw, I got this. I was riding bikes before that guy was born.' So we went riding one day and needed to cross the street. Once his back tire hit the road coming off that curb, that was it. All his body weight dropped on that seat, and he became The Lone Ranger."

George said calmly as he scratched his head, "Em, I'll tell you Son. I'm seventy-seven years old, and I've busted a nut a-many-a places…but never on a bicycle."

Frank's lips were slanted as he looked toward Nancy in evident anger. "I wish you would shut your mouth. You old, wrinkled-up, flat-nipple, slick-titty-having, hairy-legged heffa!"

Tiffany cut in to ask in shock, "Ma, you don't shave your legs?"

Before Nancy could answer, Frank spoke up. "That ain't all she don't shave. You pull those draws down, it look like she kidnapped Pam Grier down there."

George butted in. "Son, why are you concerned with a little bit of hair? The only bush that ever bothered me was in the White House."

Nancy added, "Yeah, you need to listen to your dad. Besides, they're not called draws. They're panties, Mr. Illiterate."

Frank commented bluntly, "Panties my ass! Ain't nothing feminine about all that cotton and wool shit you be wearing. I be laying there trying to spoon, and my stomach be just as itchy." Frank then turned to face us while explaining, "The worst though, is when she forgets to put a sheet in the dryer. Them draws be shocking the hell out of my stomach." Nancy was about to respond, but their argument was cut short by the doorbell.

CHAPTER 3
Solo's Services

Frank and Nancy stood in the back of the living room, staring at each other silently in anger, while Uncle Al came walking out of the bathroom. The smell was so awful, it caused us to pinch our nostrils and push our lips up in disgust.

The doorbell rang again. Uncle Al swiftly walked to the door to greet his son with great joy. After they hugged and forcefully patted each other on the back, Chris asked, "What's that smell? Y'all cooking chitterlings in here?" George told Chris that smell came from his dad, as we continued to greet him and welcome him home.

Chris was slightly taller than his dad and had a large amount of tattoos and facial hair that covered his nearly bronze skin tone. The light from the ceiling fan in the living room gave a shine to his freshly shaven bald head. He was the real goofy type, always smiling for no reason.

George, who also lived with Frank, excused himself to go to his room, which was across from the garage. On the way, he passed Frank, who stood with his arms crossed in front of the kitchen bar, protecting the items he'd hidden. Tiffany and Nancy excused themselves as well after reminding Chris how good it was to see him again. Nancy then explained to Chris that she wasn't trying to be rude; she was just afraid of the mouse. Still grinning, Chris said with his deep voice, "That's cool Auntie, I understand. I have a friend who has his own pest control business. I can have him come over and handle it for you, if you want."

Nancy looked back at Frank, who dropped his arms in excitement and began to walk toward us while shouting, "Hell yeah! You might be all right with me Klepto."

Chris giggled. "Oh boy, come on Unc. You still calling me that?"

"Yeah, until you prove me wrong," Frank said.

Uncle Al, Chris, Frank, and I were watching the college bowl games in the living room. When I noticed a tattoo on Chris's neck, I thought it was cool because it was about something we had in common. "Hey Chris, I didn't know you liked to fish. I do too."

Chris's eyes were squeezed together as he glanced at Uncle Al and Frank, then finally back at me in confusion. "I don't. What made you say that?"

Now puzzled, I began to frown up as I wondered, "Well, you have a tattoo on your neck that says 'The Reelist'?"

Chris chuckled as he explained, "Naw, that means I'm the realist out here on these streets."

My mouth almost dropped to the floor; I couldn't believe he was walking around with a misspelled tattoo on his neck. I felt like I had to say something, so I spoke cautiously, trying not to offend him. "Oh, well…um, you know it's misspelled don't you?"

Even with his goofy demeanor, Chris tried to look hard by tightening his face to say, "You know, we didn't have the luxury of Googling something whenever we wanted to on the inside."

Uncle Al asked Chris to turn his head so that he could see it, while Frank and I shook our heads in disbelief. I thought to myself: *How can you get a tattoo on your neck, saying that you're "The Reelist" on the streets, while you're locked up?*

Uncle Al was still excited about seeing his son. To initiate dialogue with him, Uncle Al asked about where he was staying and how he was able to make it over to Frank's house. Chris told him that he took the bus to get there and that he was currently staying with a lady who he'd written letters back and forth with while he was in prison.

I was starting to doze off on the couch when the doorbell rang. My eyes popped open to see the oversized clock above the TV read 7:15 p.m. on the dot. Uncle Al and Chris were now watching *Friday After Next*, while Frank got up, mumbling, "I don't know who this is. I ain't expecting nobody, and Teresa got a key to get in." Frank then looked through the peephole and popped his head back, which was followed by him whispering aggressively, "Y'all cut that TV off and come here."

Frank left the door and reached beneath the couch to grab his gun. Chris looked through the peephole, then ran to the kitchen to grab a knife. After Uncle Al glanced through the peephole, he took out his pocketknife, unfolded it, and then posted up on the wall behind the door. While I got up to peep through the hole, Chris had come back to the door with a chef knife in his right hand. He stood sideways at the crack of the door with his left hand free and ready to attack. When I looked, I saw a young, dark-skinned man with dreadlocks, and lips black enough to smoke tree bark. What was alarming though, was that he kept his right hand behind his back while using his left hand to ring the doorbell again. Without a weapon, I clenched my fists tight and slightly bent my knees as I stood to the rear of Chris, ready to pounce directly behind him.

With his gun in his right hand, hanging alongside his thigh, Frank used his left hand to yank the door open. The unforeseen, sudden movement made the young man drop the flowers he had behind his back. Chris attacked him, grabbing his collar with his left hand and pointing his knife with his right. "Whoa bro, whoa!" the young man said in a surfer-style voice. Uncle Al told Chris to put the knife down and let him go. Chris complied.

While hiding his gun in his right hand behind the door, Frank explained to the young man, "You have to excuse my nephew. He's institutionalized."

Abruptly, we heard Nancy's door close upstairs and saw her walk down the stairs, wearing a black evening dress with red lipstick and her hair done up nicely. She looked hotter than a scratched-off serial number. Frank asked, "What the hell is going on here?"

The young man said, "I'm here to pick up my matchmaker.com date, Nancy."

I looked up at Nancy, standing halfway down the stairs. "You look nice Ma."

Frank looked at me, agitated, then took his gun from behind the door and held it on display by his side as he began to walk around saying, "Oh, look at you Nancy, went and got a date with a young man. Let me ask you something boy. How old are you?"

The young man said he was twenty-three years old before Frank continued, "*Twenty-three years old*! That's it? Let me tell you something. That woman right there is fifty-five years old. She looks good now, but you don't want all that in your life. See, at fifty-five she coming at you with all types of issues and needs. The first need is a place to stay, 'cause she sure as hell ain't staying here while seeing anybody. Then she got medical bills, car payment, car insurance, credit card debt, diabetes. Now you got to make sure she stays on track with the medication schedule, 'cause sometimes she forgets. You don't want all that in your life at twenty-three." There was a seemingly long pause as everyone watched him pace back and forth in the foyer while talking. "Twenty-three years old. Em. Boy, that woman got pubic hairs older than you! I know she does too, 'cause they're gray. I see 'em all the time, in my bed and in my washcloths. Is that the life you want at twenty-three! Huh? Ask yourself! Do you want to wake up in your bed, thinking one of the stray neighborhood cats snuck under the sheets with you?!"

The young man panicked. "I'm sorry sir. I didn't realize she was seeing anyone. Her matchmaker.com profile said she was single."

Frank responded by saying, "How about I be a matchmaker and set your ass on fire if you don't get off my front porch."

Frank then closed the door shut, and we heard the young man's car pull off.

Nancy stood at the top of the stairs, screaming, "That was wrong Frank! You said we are single, so let me be single! That's my third date you've done that to."

"If by single, you mean dating, then yes," Frank said. "You can date as much as you want when you move out. But you are single though. He was just an all-time low for you, literally. The boy was twenty-three."

"Yes, but Frank, we were married for so long, I'm not looking for anything serious. I just want to have some fun and learn new things," Nancy explained.

Frank was offended, looking Nancy up and down as he argued, "What you mean? I teach you new things all the time. Just the other day, I taught you how to change a flat tire."

Nancy was annoyed. "No you didn't. I changed that flat tire! All you did was sit in the passenger seat and watch me through the side mirror. Sticking your head out the window to yell at me when I did something wrong." Nancy regathered her thoughts. "Anyway, like I was saying, I just want to have fun. He had pictures of him surfing, and—"

Frank cut her off boldly. "Surfing! Nah Nancy, you too old for that. Plus, with all that dead skin on the bottom of your feet, you'll probably cut somebody's board in half."

Nancy raised her voice. "Feet! ... Feet! You of all people want to talk about feet, with your hard, black toenails that be cutting holes in all your socks. Every time we go over somebody's house who asks us to take our shoes off at the door, you fake sick." Nancy began to mock Frank. "'Cough, cough. I need to go home Nancy. I don't feel too good.'"

George came walking out of his room with his watch rattling, as Nancy went stomping back into hers. George asked, "Y'all still going at it, huh?"

"It's a long story Pop," Frank answered.

George wondered, "What y'all doing out here? Y'all got more weapons than I had in Vietnam."

"That's an even longer story," Frank stated, as everyone began to put away their weapons.

George had showered and changed clothes. He appeared dapper in his three-piece suit and shirt-and-tie set. We all gave him a hard time about being dressed up, and he enjoyed it. I noticed he had a cigar next to his handkerchief, so I asked its purpose. George said, "Back in my day Stuart, when a man and a woman did what came naturally, the man smoked a nice cigar afterward. Then, if the time and location allowed, a little bit to drink too. I bought this cigar when I became a deacon, with tonight in mind. Before I leave, Frank call my phone, because I can't find it." As it rang, everyone in the room walked ear first toward Chris.

"My bad Mr. George. That phone looks just like mine," Chris said with a smile.

Frank nodded. "You still Klepto."

After George received his phone back from Chris, Uncle Al wanted to know, "Where you headed Mr. George?"

"To pick up Sister Patterson for our date. Hopefully, Sister Patterson will let me pat that ass."

I spoke up, puzzled. "Wait a minute. What about earlier when you were telling me all that stuff about friendship and love?"

George replied, "Yeah, but I also said I got married because of booty." We all laughed with George as he left the house in excitement.

The time was nearing eight o'clock. Uncle Al, Chris, and I were all dozing off in the living room with ESPN on TV, serving as white noise in the background. Not long ago, Tiffany had left her mother's room to go sleep in our room directly next door. Frank stood in the kitchen, making a sandwich, when Angel came out of Nancy's room and walked downstairs to get a glass of water. Frank handed Angel a bottled water, and Chris groggily shouted with a smirk, "Hey! Come here and give me a hug baby girl." Angel gave Chris a hug, and he went on talking about how tall she had gotten. The front door then became unlocked from the outside. It was Teresa. She had come back to grab her jacket, she said they would be going to eat ice cream outside a little later. Angel's face was lit with excitement, followed by her begging for permission to go. Chris greeted Teresa with an uncontainable smile and bear hug.

He told her how good she looked and how much he had missed her before she ran up the stairs.

With her jacket in hand, Teresa came downstairs from her room, which was the first of the three doors. Frank then asked, "Teresa, where's your muscular mistress?"

Teresa shook her head and laughed. "She's just my friend Dad, but she's in the truck."

Chris's eyes popped open. "You have a friend in the car? Let me go check her out."

He took a few steps toward the door before Frank and Uncle Al said in unison, "Don't waste your time." Chris stopped in his tracks, then looked at me with his eyes slanted inward, questioning what he had just heard from his dad and uncle. Without speaking, I kept my eyes on Chris as I dropped my head and shook it in concurrence with Frank and Uncle Al.

Chris stood at the end of the couch next to his dad, who was sitting, and spoke loud enough for us all to hear him. "Come on y'all, she can't be that bad," he said lightheartedly.

Uncle Al said, "Naw Son, your uncle Frank right about this one." Uncle Al raised his voice to ask, "Hey Teresa, what you say that girl's nickname was again? Wasn't it like Silverback, or Boulder Shoulders, or something like that?"

Teresa agreed, "Oh yeah, the guys at the BBQ Pit call her The Broad Broad."

After Chris heard that, he threw both his hands up in surrender as he flopped on the couch adjacent to his dad, mumbling, "Naw, I'm alright. I'll let that one go."

After she nudged me on the arm, I looked down at Angel. She was looking up at me with big eyes and her neck stretched out, silently asking for permission to go with her aunt Teresa. Teresa stood at the front door, pleading, "Yes Angel! Hurry up! Let's go!"

I told Angel she could go, then I gave her a hug and twenty dollars for whatever ice cream or snacks she wanted while she was out. She had put on her boots and run to the door beside Teresa when I said, "Angel, make sure you're back before Santa Claus gets here. You don't want him to see you."

The room was quiet. Teresa and Angel both looked back at me without even a hint of a smile. They both said good-bye as Teresa opened the door for Angel to walk out first. I overheard Teresa rhetorically ask Angel, "What are you asking him for? You don't need permission from a man to do nothing. All you're doing is feeding his ego. I'm your aunt, and I said you could go. Now come on."

Furiously, I ran to the door. Teresa was halfway out when I yanked the doorknob out of her hand, causing the door to open as far as it could go. Angel had already made it to the truck when I started to yell at Teresa with my fists balled and eyes piercing with rage, "What the hell wrong with you?! Don't you ever disrespect me in front of my daughter like that!"

Teresa replied calmly, with a disingenuous smile, "Whoa, calm down Stuart. I won't disrespect you in front of your daughter.

But the last time I checked, she wasn't your daughter." Then she grabbed the doorknob out of my hand and closed the door as she left.

I stood in the foyer for a while to calm down and collect my thoughts. Chris, Uncle Al, and Frank all looked away, pretending they hadn't seen or heard what just happened. I began to think. *Technically, she was right. Angel isn't my biological daughter. If she were, I would've been outside yanking her out of that truck, ice cream or no ice cream. My issue wasn't with Angel though. It was with Teresa and her lack of respect for men, and in particular, me. If she were Angel's uncle, I would've took it outside. I couldn't do that though, because she's Angel's aunt.*

I needed to find a way to at least be cordial with Teresa for the rest of my time in California. Since working on things helps me to relax and think, I decided to fix the doorknob. I'd noticed it was loose when I yanked it earlier. Once I saw that it was two flat-head screws that had come loose, I grabbed a dime out of my pocket and began to tighten them. I could hear Frank approach me from the side, followed by him peeking over my shoulder, asking curiously, "Hey uh…Stuart. How'd you learn that lil trick, to use a coin if you don't have a screwdriver?"

I stood up to answer. "Oh, one time I was watching this video on Y—" Frank's eyes got big as he looked at me. I quickly remembered Tiffany telling me that Frank hated YouTube, so I improvised. "You know, I uh…saw it on a videotape, when I was a kid."

Frank displayed an excited smile while pointing his index fingers and thrusting his head forward. "I knew it! I knew it! I keep telling people, everything they need to know is on them tapes. Don't nobody need no YouTube." Uncle Al and Chris looked back at Frank like he was crazy. I nodded my head and verbally agreed with him so that he would stop talking about it. Then Uncle Al and Chris started looking at me like I was crazy too.

Not long after, Uncle Al and Chris both stood up, and Uncle Al asked me to take him to his hotel because he was getting sleepy. Chris told Frank that he would be coming back tonight with his prison friend, Solo, who now owned his own pest control business. After Frank expressed that he had no issues with that, Uncle Al and Chris made their way to the door. You could hear a subtle clunking sound as they approached. Frank stopped everything. "Hold it! Klepto, pull up your pant legs."

Chris nagged, "Come on Unc. You don't trust me, even a lil bit?"

Uncle Al took Chris's side. "Frank, the boy been here on the couch the whole time. Give him a break."

Frank responded to Uncle Al, "Al, I know that's your son, but you been in South Carolina for a while now. Listen, I know that boy, and I know he got something up his pant leg too."

Uncle Al was too sleepy to argue, so he asked Chris, "Chris, gone pull up your pant legs so your uncle can look silly."

Chris wore gray, loose-fitting sweatpants on top of his black air force ones. Reluctantly, Chris pulled up his pant legs, and I couldn't make out what was pressed against his leg.

Frank had no issues in determining what it was as he shouted, "Is that my Tombstone?!" Klepto Chris had stolen a personal-sized frozen pizza, and with it still in the box, tried to stuff it in his sock. Frank said while pointing, "I told you. That's the Klepto Chris I know."

"Why were you stealing a frozen pizza?" Uncle Al asked.

Chris was thinking on his toes when he replied, "Oh, well, I uh…was going to feed the homeless." I personally thought Chris was a horrible liar to be such a renowned thief; the two usually go hand-in-hand.

Frank turned his lips and shrugged his shoulders carelessly. "You know what? Keep the pizza Klepto. Merry Christmas."

He couldn't believe it. "What? Are you serious Unc?"

Frank nodded before he spoke. "Yeah, that's the least I could do. You know, with you giving me the hookup on the exterminator and all."

"Cool. Thanks Unc. I appreciate it," Chris said, then turned to face the door, beelining his way past me and out of the house. On the way out, he patted me on the back and said, "Hurry up Stu! I need to sit down. My leg got numb from that frozen pizza."

Once outside, I asked Chris how he'd even managed to steal a frozen pizza. He told me he grabbed it when he went to the kitchen for the knife.

I dropped Uncle Al off at the hotel near the airport and headed to Chris's friend Solo's house. Solo lived in Compton. His house was easy to find, in large part because of the extermination van that was parked in the driveway, blocking the sidewalk, but also because of the large amount of guys sitting on the front porch. After putting the car in park and seeing some of the guys stand up on the porch, obviously looking at my rental car, I said to Chris, "I thought you said his nickname was Solo."

Chris answered, "Yeah, it is. That's because of the cup though. He likes to hang out with his boys."

"Yeah, I can tell." Chris wanted to know if I wanted to come in. I told him no, and that I would meet him back at the house later.

I answered no for a couple reasons. First, because that porch full of thugs was intimidating. I wasn't used to seeing that where I lived. I knew they were thugs too, not only from what Chris had told me about them, but also because it was dark outside and they all had shades on. The second, and most important reason was because I had on a T-shirt that I won at a Dick's Sporting Goods fishing tournament a while ago. Although it had a fish on it, the back of the T-shirt said Fishing Dick's. The last thing I wanted was for a group of ex-cons to see me from the back and then read that I'm Fishing Dick's.

It was nearly nine thirty when I arrived back at my in-laws' house. I brought in our luggage and put it in our room, which was packed with VHS tapes at every turn. Frank sat at the kitchen bar, drinking some type of liquor and watching the television from a distance.

Now sitting at the bar with Frank, I asked him why he had so many VHS tapes in that bedroom. Frank replied, "My agent told me that I needed to order a new shipment because tapes are coming back soon. If you think about it Stu, he's right. All the fash-ion comes back around, all the music comes back around. Really, everything, when you think about it. People always say history repeats itself, so why wouldn't it be the same way with tapes?"

There was a long moment of silence as I looked back at him, trying to think of a clear answer, before I avoided the question altogether by asking, "Does your agent get a cut of every tape you buy?"

Frank answered, "Yeah, not much though. Maybe forty percent." Simultaneously, the doorbell rang as I thought to myself, *That explains why.*

After seeing that it was Chris and his friends, I opened the door. Chris introduced us to Solo and the two guys who worked under him, called Roach and Big Ant. With those names, to me it sounded like they were the ones that needed to be exterminated. They all stood about the same size, wearing a variation of khaki suits. Now in the house, their shades were never removed. Which, for me, only confirmed what I'd thought earlier about them being thugs.

Following the introductions, Chris walked to the kitchen to heat up his frozen pizza. I noticed none of them had tools of any sort on their person, so I asked if they needed to run back to their van for anything. Unlike Chris, these guys didn't smile at all. Solo simply lifted the grocery bag of items he had in his hand, answering, "Nope. Mice are simple. Everything I need is right here."

Big Ant, who stood behind Solo's left shoulder, nudged him. Solo then said, "Oh I forgot, I'm gonna need a beer too."

I wondered, "Uh, what do you need a beer for?"

Solo explained to us that mice are more likely to drink beer, as opposed to water, to activate the poison. Frank questioned, "So what type of beer do mice like?"

Big Ant spoke up. "Oh, they like any kind of forty ounce." The tone in which he said it made him sound excited, which in turn made me a bit skeptical.

Frank responded to him by saying, "That's a thirsty-ass mouse ain't it? Well, I haven't had a forty since '91. I have some Angry Orchard hard cider if that'll work?"

I thought I heard Big Ant mumble under his breath, "Don't nobody want that crap." I wasn't sure though, because Solo was speaking at the same time, saying, "Yes, hard cider should be fine."

I passed them the bottle, then sat beside Chris at the bar while he ate his pizza. From a distance, I watched the guys set up two mouse stations near the garage door, with Frank looking over their shoulders. In the grocery bag were four ashtrays and two Ziploc bags. One bag had a liquid-type substance in it; the other had poison. Each station had an ashtray full of poison and an ashtray with a small amount of cider in it. There was only a small amount of cider in each tray because, like anticipated, Big Ant started drinking it himself. What was weird though, was that he was talking to the ashtrays like they were his drinking buddies. Big Ant said,

"Here's a sip for you, and now a gulp for me." The cider was done after that, so he handed the bottle to Frank, who walked toward the kitchen, where I was, to throw it away.

I met him halfway to create distance between me and Chris, who still sat at the bar. I whispered in Frank's ear, "You don't think this seems a little sketchy? Excluding Chris, you got three ex-cons in here, and only one of them is working. One of them trying to get drunk, and the other one…" I paused to look up. What I saw made me tell Frank, "Turn around and look at this." Frank and I stood at the edge of the kitchen, facing the hallway. We were watching Roach use his brush in the hallway mirror to tighten up his prison part.

In case you don't know, a prison part is when you use a brush to move your hair in opposite directions until a part forms. Guys usually do this when they don't have a legitimate barber available who can cut a part for them, ideally in prison. Then, once you're done brushing, the part is usually topped with a bunch of gel-like grease and either a stocking cap or a do-rag to hold it in place. They don't want to lose all that progress they made before burning their forearms out while brushing.

Frank whispered back in my ear, "It's fine Stuart. See, that's what's wrong with your generation today. Y'all don't trust nobody. These men paid their debt to society and are out here making a honest living. They're OK."

I nodded slowly, with my lips up as if to signal, "OK, fair enough." Solo then yelled from the hallway, asking Frank to bring him two paper towels for the liquid.

The way Solo explained it to Frank was that this liquid was something that he and Roach had created when they had a mouse problem in prison. What you are supposed to do is soak the paper towel in the liquid and then put the two ashtrays on top of it. Apparently, when the mouse goes to eat and steps on the napkin, it causes a hard substance to form on the bottom of its feet for up to forty-eight hours. That's important, so that we can hear where it's at. In addition to that though, it will track where he goes for the next hour because of the small ink deposits in the liquid. That is equally important to us; now we would know where to look when it died.

As they were wrapping things up to go, Roach asked Chris how they were doing on time. Chris pulled out his phone and told them that it was ten forty-five and then put his phone back in his pocket. From sitting next to him, I was able to see that his screen saver was a picture of Tiffany and Angel. With a smile, I asked, "Man, you really love your cousin don't you? I saw your screen saver."

Chris giggled as he answered, "Yeah Stu, you know family is all we got."

I agreed with him before I stood up to walk the guys to the door. I felt around in my pocket and couldn't find my phone. Then, after a quick thought, I snapped, "Klepto! Give me my dag-gone phone back!" He quickly handed it to me, trying to explain himself before I cut him off, still angry. "I don't want to hear it Klepto!" Then we met with the rest of the guys at the front door.

Frank had begun a spiel on how he felt about them. They all looked at him with admiration as he spoke, "I was telling my son-in-law earlier how proud I am of you young black men. You paid your debt to society, and now you're out here making an honest living for yourself. If don't nobody else tell you, I'm proud of you, and keep up the good work." They all said thank you, including Chris, which grabbed Frank's attention briefly, but Frank just ignored Chris. Frank used the wall to press against while writing a check to pay them, when he asked, "So where did you guys learn this trade at? What school did you all go to?" Frank handed Solo the check as the three of them began to look at each other, clueless as how to answer Frank's question.

While scratching his prison part, Roach said, "We didn't go to no school. We learned all this on YouTube."

Right away, Frank raised his voice and pointed toward the door. "Get the HELL out of my house!" Since Chris was the last one out the door, he shut it behind himself.

———

It was four o'clock on Christmas morning. I reached for Tiffany but got nothing except pillow. I was confused for a bit as to where she may have been. She was in bed with me when I fell asleep. Tiffany abruptly pushed the door open. When I saw her, I started smiling like a preacher during offering. The smile quickly left though, when she started talking to me with attitude in her voice. "Stuart! Where is Angel?"

Although I was offended, I didn't want to yell back at her because I still wanted her to come to bed. So I answered in a calm, soothing voice, "I don't know. She should be back by now. She left with Teresa and that hulk woman to go get some ice cream last night."

She never budged verbally or physically as she stood at the doorway. "Well she's not here. I checked all downstairs, my mom's room, and Teresa's room. Did you give her a time to come back?"

"Yeah. I told her to be back before Santa gets here."

"What! She's almost sixteen years old. She knows there is no Santa."

My eyes popped open as I frowned my lips, saying, "Oh," like I was shocked to hear how old she was. I was getting to be as bad as my dad when it came to remembering people's ages. Then Tiffany's phone beeped from a text. After she read it, she held her phone close to her chest and leaned against the doorframe of the bedroom, exhaling, "Oh, thank God." She caught her breath, then explained to me that she had texted her sister, asking about Angel. Her sister had just texted her back, saying that she was with them still. Angel had fallen asleep on Brittany's couch, and they'd decided just to spend the night there.

Now that that was over, I groaned, "Thank God," as I rolled on my back.

Tiffany asked curiously, "Uh, what are you doing?"

Trying to make my voice deep, I sounded like a radio host on a R&B station as I answered softly, "Well I was hoping we could get started early on a Merry Christmas."

Tiffany's attitude came back like it had never left. "Oh, *now* you want to spend time with me. You hardly said two words to me since we've been at my parents' house. Then you didn't stand up for me on the plane, you made fun of Angel's boyfriend and embarrassed her, and now my innocent teenage daughter is spending the night with lesbians because of you."

I wanted to tell her that her daughter wasn't so innocent, based off that conversation I'd overheard in the airport between her and her boyfriend. I could've argued a lot more things too, but at this point I just wanted to have quiet time with my wife. "You know what? I'm sorry. Come to bed so we can talk about it," I said.

She knew me too well though. "No. You don't mean that. You only said that because you want me to come to bed. I'm going to sleep in my mom's room." Tiffany turned her back to me and walked out the door.

It couldn't have been more than thirty minutes later, while I was lying there texting unanswered sad faces to Tiffany, that I heard footsteps creeping up the stairs. I had been up ever since Tiffany walked out of the room earlier, and I'd never heard the front door open. At first, I was alarmed that it might have been one of those ex-cons, coming back to burglarize us. I sat up in my bed to listen closer, as the footsteps passed my room and the owner of the footsteps began knocking on Nancy's door.

"Who is it?" Nancy answered.

Apparently, I wasn't the only one who was lonely. Frank whispered, "It's me. Come on, let me in."

"You got to be kidding me," Nancy said. "With the way you've been talking to me and treating me lately…go back to your room Frank!"

Frank responded with, "Come on now Nancy. We're getting too old for this. Besides, it's Christmas."

Nancy's frustration was growing by the second. "Frank, I don't care if it was the day of Jesus's return! You ain't getting no loving from me."

I don't know how Tiffany remained so quiet; I thought this was hilarious. Then again, she had always been a deeper sleeper than me. She continued, "Frank, you need to go start breakfast. You know everybody will be up early since it's Christmas."

Frank walked past my room and down the stairs mumbling, "This don't make no sense. Everybody around here getting some except me."

CHAPTER 4
Arts and Crafts

After taking my shower, I could smell the bacon throughout the house. I got dressed and went downstairs to eat. The house was so cold, I thought I was visiting dead people. Frank was still downstairs in the kitchen by himself, cooking, when I approached him with a fist bump. "Good morning Mr. Frank."

He continued to stir the waffle mix batter while looking up to say, "Speak for yourself."

I smiled with my arms open wide, pretending I didn't know what was bothering him, as I said in a convincing tone, "Come on Frank. It's Christmas. Let the Yuletide be gay."

He responded, "My daughter already gay. Ain't that enough?"

I chuckled a bit while taking a seat at the bar and nibbling on some bacon since the rest of the food wasn't ready yet. I looked toward the living room and noticed Frank had put up the Christmas tree. It was a small, white tree that stood about five feet, but it didn't have any decorations on it, not even a star. After I asked about it, Frank said, "I leave the decorations for Nancy. That used to be her big thing. Not so much now though."

I nodded slowly to signal that I understood before saying, "You know Tiffany never told me how y'all met."

By now, the bacon and grits were done, and he was waiting on the Belgian waffles to finish before doing the eggs last. Since the waffle maker made a beeping sound when it was done, he turned to face me as he said, "You know, I really don't remember when or how we met because we went to school together for so long. I do remember when we started seeing each other though. That night, she came to my apartment and watched some infomercial on TV, then decided to quit birth control, smoking, and pork all on the same day."

"Yeah, I remember Tiffany telling me how her mom likes to eat healthy and organic stuff."

Frank continued to speak. "Yeah, but I was worried about the birth control part. She told me I didn't have nothing to worry about. We could just have sex when she wasn't ovulating. I asked her, 'How in the hell am I going to keep track of something I can't even spell?'"

I told him I wasn't any better; I thought he was talking about that chocolate powder stuff.

Frank went on to tell me, "So we did that for about a month or two, but I was still scared. So I called to break up with her, and that's when she told me she was pregnant with Tiffany. I was young and dumb, so I still wanted to break up with her. My dad wouldn't let me though, thank God. He told me one of the worst things I could ever do is let my child grow up without a father. Like I said, I couldn't see it then. Looking back on it now though, sticking with her is probably the best decision I ever made. My daughters turned out to be great: one is a psychologist, and the other owns a hair salon. Now granted, one of them is dating a polar bear, and the other one married you, but they're doing OK."

I chuckled a bit before commenting, "Oh, I didn't know Teresa owned her own hair salon."

"Yeah, she owns that shop right around the corner over there," Frank said.

After quick thought, I asked, "Oh, you talking about that salon we drove past in downtown?"

Frank blurted out, "Naw, in the garage over there, right around the corner from the stairway."

I laughed at his comment while wondering, "So why did y'all divorce then?"

The waffle maker beeped, and he was in the process of filling it with more batter as he spoke up. "Hm. Joint accounts! Before we had joint accounts, my credit was so good, I could've lied to Jesus. Now, I can't even get a tank of gas on credit. As soon as I put my card in the pump, the screen says, 'Please pay inside.'"

Frank had me rolling when he said that. Then he closed the waffle maker again to finish speaking, "Seriously though, she took forty thousand dollars out of our savings and started her own business, Nancy's Fish Fry and fuckin' Yoga Studio, and ain't tell me nothing. Then to top it off, when the business failed, like I said it would, she gone tell me." Frank began to imitate Nancy's voice as he spoke, "'Don't worry about it Frank, I'ma put the money back. I just got a part-time job at the gas station.'" After Frank saw my jaw drop and my eyes expand in shock, he told me that was the same reaction he had when Nancy told him.

I shook my head while saying, "Wow Mr. Frank. It takes a big man to let her come back after all that."

He groaned. "Yeah, well, besides the fact that she's a good tax write-off, I stay true to my vows." After I asked what he had meant by that, he explained, "After our divorce, we lived apart for about four years. She ended up burning through whatever money she had saved up. That little bit of alimony she was getting from me wasn't enough to cover all her expenses. I knew she had nowhere else to go since her parents passed away a few years ago, and her only sibling, Sabrina, is living with her boyfriend. I took her back because that's what I'm supposed to do. I made a vow of, 'For better or for worse, as long as we both shall live, period.' There were no caveats in there that said unless anything."

I nodded my head. "I agree."

Frank ended our conversation with, "Now, she can talk all that crap about me if she wants to, but she was the one who filed for divorce. I don't believe in it."

I agreed with Frank by saying, "Me either."

The time was now six thirty. Frank had just finished washing and putting away the Belgian waffle iron and was now in the process of pulling out two dozen eggs from the refrigerator. We heard the locks on the door move and the sound of soft, slow footsteps travel across the hardwood floor. I looked back and saw George in his three-piece suit, walking toward us. With his buttons undone, the suit was hanging off of him, and the cigar he had brought with him was broken in half. "Hey, good morning Mr. George. Merry Christmas," I said with enthusiasm.

George stood at the end of the bar between Frank and me while he spoke. "Yeah, I wish I could say that it was, but I couldn't seal the deal." After he said that, I felt like the three of us had become a circle of unintentional celibates. George explained, "Sister Patterson been reading some book that tells her she supposed to wait ninety days before she lets me have sex. I told her I'm seventy-seven years old. I can't guarantee I'll be around for the next ninety seconds. I asked her if they have a senior citizen section in that book. I can understand ninety days if you're thirty or forty, but at seventy-seven, you asking for way too much."

Frank took a break from cracking the eggs as we both laughed, and I asked, "So what happened to your cigar?"

George told us that the cigar broke while he was trying to get comfortable on her couch. George then asked us, "What were y'all talking about before I walked over?"

"Frank, I didn't tell you this, but Tiffany and I haven't been talking to each other lately," I said. "She's mad at me for something else again. I swear, it feels like I can't do nothing right. So before you walked up, Frank was telling me how him and Nancy got to be where they are now and how he keeps his vows."

George's head snapped back. "So let me get this straight. Have you tried to talk to her?"

"Yes."

George abruptly questioned, "But you were trying to get some booty when you did, weren't you?"

I felt like this old man could read me like a book when I replied, "Yes, but all the stuff she's mad at me about isn't technically my fault."

George put his head down and shook it in disappointment as he mumbled something under his breath. I couldn't make out what it was, so after I asked him to speak up, he told me, "TV baby! That's what I said. TV has been making men look so dumb and insensitive for so long, we're starting to act like it. Listen to me Stuart, it doesn't matter if you're right, wrong, or indifferent. You have to break the ice and go talk to your wife. You know why?" With my eyes wide open in an uninterested fashion, I shook my head no, showing no concern for wanting to initiate dialogue with Tiffany. George responded by saying, "Because you are the man. See, when I was coming along, getting your feelings hurt and then not speaking to that person was something that women did, not men. A man is supposed to be the leader of the household, and the main thing a leader does is initiate." I sat back on my stool and continued to listen to George while Frank scrambled eggs in a large bowl. George interpreted himself by saying, "Think about it Stuart. You used to play football. The quarterback was your teammate, but he was also the leader. It's the same way in your marriage. Y'all are partners in life, but you lead that partnership. Because just like the quarterback gets blamed whether it's win, lose, or draw, whether your marriage sinks or swims, the only thing people will want to know is what did the man do." I rested my forearm on the bar as I nodded my head to think about it for a while. I never heard anyone say these things before, or put it in that perspective.

I said, "OK, Mr. George, I'll talk to her, and I'll make sure it's not when I'm trying to get some booty too." We all laughed before I commented, "I guess I better say something to end this drought. Since things have been shaky for the past couple days, you pretty much know we haven't been doing nothing for the past couple days either."

Frank laughed. "Boy please. You haven't seen a drought yet. Wait till she goes through menopause. I remember when Nancy got it. I had the AC blasting with a space heater beside the bed. I didn't know what she wanted."

Since the house was so cold, I wanted to ask if she still had menopause, but I didn't say anything. George was chewing on some bacon. "Shoot, menopause ain't nothing. You want to talk about a drought, my wife was sick for three and a half years before she passed last year." George saw me looking up in the air and using my fingers to count when he offered, "Let me help you with that math Stuart. It's been four and a half years since I've touched a woman."

I couldn't believe it. "What? It's been four and a half years since you've touched a woman?"

George said, "That's right."

Frank jumped in. "That's true too, 'cause in Santa Monica you're not allowed to touch the strippers." George jokingly told Frank to shut the hell up after his last comment, while we all cackled.

The eggs had just been poured in the pan when Brittany, Teresa, and Angel walked through the door. We welcomed them with mutual Christmas greetings. Teresa even gave me a cordial, "Stuart."

After looking her up and down, I returned the favor with a cordial, "Teresa." Angel gave us hugs before she and Teresa ran upstairs to Nancy's room. Brittany walked over to the bar in a camouflage hat. She had an empty Pepsi bottle in her hand that she used to spit her tobacco in. She gave us all handshakes, then confirmed with Frank that dinner would be starting at six o'clock. We all told Brittany that we looked forward to seeing her as she walked out the house, claiming to have errands to run.

I saw the door close behind Brittany, then turned to George and Frank. "That's one of the reasons why Tiffany is mad with me, because I let Angel hang out with them last night."

George said, "Yeah, I can't blame her for that one. You keep letting that girl hang out with Brittany if you want to. She gone turn Angel into Angelo."

George went to his room, and Frank was nearly done with eggs. He asked me to go upstairs and let the women know that the food was ready. I walked up the stairs and knocked on the door, yelling, "Hey y'all, breakfast is ready!"

I could hear "Christmas in Hollis" playing as Nancy yelled back, "OK, we will be down there in about an hour or so."

I didn't think anything of it, so while I was still at the top of the stairs on my way down, I hollered at Frank, "They said they would be down in about an hour or so!"

Frank lost his mind, and the spatula too I think, because I heard a bunch of metal clanging around. "What! Ain't nobody waiting no hour to eat breakfast! Stay right there Stuart, I'm coming!" he screamed. Frank stomped up the stairs past me and banged on Nancy's door. "Hey! Y'all come downstairs right now and eat this food! We ain't waiting no hour to eat!" I could hear the women giggling over the music before Frank shouted, "Don't laugh at me! Y'all the ones in there listening to Run DMC! We live in California, y'all need to be listening to N.W.A!"

Nancy turned down the music to argue, "Frank, shut up and give us a minute. Followed by me asking, "What you know about N.W.A. Mr. Frank?"

"What!" Frank was shocked that I had asked him that. "I was almost a member of N.W.A."

"For real?! I didn't know that."

Frank said, "Yea, but they told me I didn't have enough attitude. I met all the other requirements though." I couldn't help laughing at his comment before asking Frank to let me hear him rap. After saying, "yo" about twenty times like it was 1994, Frank started.

"Yo, it's big Frank, reppin' for Christmas,
I just cooked breakfast, got a sink full of dishes.

I'm sick of everybody living off my dime,
When Tiff married Stu, I said, 'About damn time!'

I wonder if Teresa will ever catch a hint,
I bet you she will, if I start charging rent.

And y'all women hurry up, you taking too long,
Left me out here with Stu, his breath smell like a thong."

I stood at the top of the stairs, leaning on the rail with both fore-arms. I stared at Frank with a straight face. I didn't find his rap to be entertaining at all. The women obviously didn't feel the same way though. I could hear them cackling through the door.

Frank turned back around and continued to bang on the door. "Come on Nancy, and open up this door! You already took four years of alimony. Now you trying to take Christmas too?"

The bedroom door slowly opened, and all the women began to walk out, with Nancy leading the way. Frank didn't budge as Nancy said, "Ain't nobody trying to take Christmas. Now, excuse me Frank so I can go eat breakfast."

Frank stood still and asked, "So what were y'all doing in there?"

"Having some girl time," Nancy said with a feminine tone while bumping Frank's shoulder to continue downstairs.

Once downstairs, we all made our plates and sat at the dining table to eat breakfast. George had come out of his room to join us. Before too long, Angel's phone rang. Tiffany took it out of her pocket to see that it was Javier. Since it was Christmas Day, Tiffany decided to give Angel her phone back and let her speak to her boy-friend. With uncontainable excitement, Angel dropped her knife and fork on her plate, causing a loud ringing sound. Angel then grabbed the phone from her mom before squeezing her neck and giving her an animated kiss on the cheek. After excusing herself from the table, Angel ran upstairs to Nancy's room and closed the door for privacy to her conversation. I didn't think that she should be getting privacy, but Tiffany said that was normal for teenage girls. So I dropped the subject.

About fifteen minutes later, at 7:00 a.m., my phone rang as well. I looked at the screen and saw that it was my brother, Shane, then I excused myself from the table and walked to the living room. While walking to the living room, I thought to myself, *Answer the phone like you're cool, 'cause you don't want him to joke you.* I started thinking of different greetings. *Hey, what's up bro?* Or maybe: *Hi brother.* I couldn't decide, and I knew I needed to answer the phone soon or I would miss the call, so I simply said, "Hey, Happy Holidays bro."

He was offended. "WHAT! Stop saying 'Happy Holidays'! It's 'Merry Christmas' boy. That's a daggone shame. You been work-ing for six years, and you still answering the phone like you on a job interview. And what is 'bro'? It's supposed to be 'bruh.' You would've known that had you stayed in public school." I shook my head and smacked my lips, knowing he would've joked me no mat-ter how I answered the phone.

Since adulthood, Shane and I haven't exchanged gifts on Christmas. We both believe that money would be better spent on the kids, who would appreciate it more. Plus, as adults, the gifts we really want, no one is going to go out and buy them for us. Out of love though, we still buy gifts for our parents. Shane and I usually just call each other with well-wishes for the holiday.

After telling me that his kids enjoyed the gifts I sent them, Shane told me that he'd just left our parents' house. I had splurged a bit this year and bought my parents smart watches. I asked Shane, "How did they like them?"

"Well, you know they both country and don't know how to use nothing," Shane said. "At least Mama has enough sense to take hers to the store to get them to set it up. Daddy already wearing his, but he don't know how to cut it on. So he said he just gonna use it as a mirror."

I grinned while saying, "Shane stop playing."

"I ain't playing. You should've saw Daddy trying to trim his goatee with that little-ass watch."

I stood in the living room, covering my mouth with my shirt, as I released a belly-wrenching laugh. Shane continued to speak. "Forget all that though. What's going on with Teresa? Does she look as good in person?"

Teresa was still eating at the dining table, so I lowered my voice to say, "There's a reason why her mouth is closed in her Facebook pics. You ever notice in all her group pics, when everyone else is smiling, she's just smirking? There's a reason for that."

Shane asked, "Her teeth jacked up?"

"Bshh, jacked up ain't the word. Her teeth spread out like the 1st and the 15th. Plus, she's already spoken for."

Shane questioned, "Oh, she got a man?"

All I could think of was how Brittany was spitting tobacco in a bottle and scratching her stomach earlier. Still whispering, I answered, "I guess you could say that." He seemed to lose all interest at that point and before long, we got off the phone with each other.

I turned around to walk back to the table and was startled a bit by Angel, who stood directly behind me, asking, "When are we going to open up the gifts?" I could tell Angel was excited, so I asked if everyone was ready to open gifts. After little discussion, they all made their way into the living room.

All of us were standing around the tree, with the exception of Tiffany and her mom, who sat underneath the tree, and George, who sat on the couch. Nancy was digging for gifts when Tiffany complimented her on her earrings. I hadn't even noticed Nancy's earrings until then. It was clear though, that she had made them herself. Nancy continued, "Thanks baby. You know, I read in a magazine that it's popular for women to wear Christmas tree orna-ments as earrings during the holidays. I found these little wooden Christmas tree–shaped ornaments at the cash register when I was leaving the hardware store. I just painted them and made them look pretty."

Tiffany's eyes were wide open as she nodded slowly. I don't think Tiffany was expecting to hear that; she was probably just trying to be nice with her previous compliment. "Oh, OK Ma. That's nice," Tiffany commented.

Frank said exactly what I was thinking. "Nancy, what kind of arts-and-crafts Christmas you got going on around here? That shit must be popular on the moon somewhere, 'cause I sure as hell ain't seen nobody in California wearing no damn ornaments as earrings."

Nancy put him down fast. "Frank shut up! Instead of talking about making earrings, we can talk about making U-turns again. Is that what you want?"

Frank took two steps back and started shaking his head while scratching it. "Naw, I'm alright."

Nancy finished, "Like I was saying, I'm glad you like them 'cause I made a pair for you and Angel." Nancy then told them Merry Christmas as she handed each one a small box with wooden Christmas tree–shaped ornaments inside. It sounded like some- one was forcing Tiffany to say thank you, but she did it either way. Tiffany nudged Angel to do the same. Reluctantly, she also thanked her grandma. Nancy's face had a huge smile on it as she stood up to squeeze Tiffany and Angel with each arm in a group hug. Angel and Tiffany just gave her pats on the back.

Frank saw how disengaged Angel appeared to be then said, "Angel, don't get upset baby. That's what broke people do on Christmas—make shit." George and I couldn't help but laugh.

Teresa gave her parents, George, and Angel Starbucks gift cards. Apparently, like Shane and me, Tiffany and Teresa didn't exchange gifts either.

After Nancy handed Frank a box wrapped in Christmas paper, Frank looked me in the eye while resting his hand on my shoulder. "Stuart, I want you to know that all of us chipped in to get you this, but it was my idea. Man-to-man, I think it's something you're going to really like." I got nervous when he said the gift was his idea. I remembered Tiffany telling me how he was notorious for giving people gifts they couldn't use but were perfect for him.

I grabbed the box and opened it as everyone looked at me, smiling with anticipation. It was professional hair clippers. I smiled and said, "Wow! Thank y'all, these are really nice."

Frank pointed at me with a grin. "See, I knew you'd like them."

"Yeah, I can see why everyone had to chip in on these," I responded. "A pair of clippers like this isn't cheap."

Now sitting on the floor again, Nancy spoke up in a sympathetic voice. "Well, that's because my baby loves her husband, and we love our son-in-law."

I replied, "Thank you. I love y'all too, and I'm thankful for the clippers." I was hesitant to continue, but I felt like it needed to be said. "Um, I don't know if y'all noticed it or not, but I'm bald."

There was an awkward moment of silence as everyone looked at Frank, scratching his head before saying, "Dang, and I threw the receipt away too. I guess I'm just gonna have to use these to tighten myself up every now and again. Sorry about that Stuart."

I looked at him out of the corner of my eye, knowing this was done on purpose. "Yeah. No problem Mr. Frank. I guess you're just gonna have to do that."

Teresa almost blew me away when she asked her parents if they were going to exchange gifts. Frank looked up and pointed to the ceiling. After Nancy saw that, she explained, "Your dad says since I'm living here, he's already giving me the gift of shelter. So we don't exchange gifts."

George asked, "What about me? I'm your father."

Frank looked up and pointed to the ceiling again.

Teresa commented, "But wait a minute Daddy. I might live here, but I'm still your daughter."

"What!" Frank said. "With the way you and Brittany be raiding my refrigerator..." He cut himself off to point one finger straight in the air toward the ceiling, and used the other hand to point toward the refrigerator. Frank then turned to Tiffany to hand her a gift. She ripped it open with enthusiasm. It was a VHS tape showcasing African American divas such as Billie Holiday, Ella Fitzgerald,

Aretha Franklin, Diana Ross, etc. Tiffany had a puzzled look on her face. Frank explained, "Your mama told me how you like the *Golden Girls*, so I figured this was right up your alley."

Tiffany smacked her lips. "Yes Dad, I like the TV show *Golden Girls*."

Frank said, "Oh, I'm sorry about that Tiff. I guess I'll…"

Tiffany cut him off. "No no no, no no no. Don't worry about it Dad. I will keep it, watch it, and love it. Thank you, and Merry Christmas."

I saw Frank turn his head and mumble with his fists balled, "Shoot!" I knew he really wanted that VHS tape for himself.

Tiffany and I had decided to buy gifts jointly this year. She would buy for her parents and say it was from us, and I would buy for Angel and say it was from us. I thought Tiffany was trying to get her parents back together with the gift she had bought. It was two gift cards: one to a steak house and one to a movie theater. What ended up happening was: Frank took the gift card to the steak house, and Nancy took the gift card to the movies. They obviously didn't think anything of it, but I could tell it bothered Tiffany. She turned to face me, struggling to keep a smile on her face and nearly breaking down in tears.

To help Tiffany out by getting the attention off of her, I apologized to George for not having a gift for him. I told him that we didn't know while we were out shopping that he would be here. George put his hand up as he sat on the couch, shaking his head, telling me that it was OK and he understood.

After thanking George for being so understanding, I turned to face Angel. Her two boxes were at the front of the tree, so I pointed to them for her to open. When the gifts were opened, Angel stared at Tiffany and me with her eyes slanted inward and chin pulled back in disappointed shock. This made Tiffany stop crying. She nudged me on the forearm and whispered in my ear with aggression, "Stuart! She is fifteen years old! Why would you get her Barbie dolls and a Little Mermaid lunchbox?"

I appeared dumbfounded. I was at a loss for words. I didn't know what to get Angel. She didn't give me any recommendations, and every time I see her, all she does is play on her cell phone. Tiffany tried to make up for my gift by telling Angel, "Don't worry Angel, we left the rest of your gifts in Maryland. You'll get them when we get home." Now I was the one looking at Tiffany in shock and discreetly shaking my head in disagreement.

George wasn't any better though. He bought Angel some barrettes and a pacifier, claiming he forgot how old she was. That was the only person George bought a gift for too. He was firm when he said, "I don't buy gifts for grown people. Y'all work every day, and I'm on a fixed income." Nobody could argue with George on that one.

Knowing that the only gifts left to give were from Frank to Angel and from me to Tiffany, I turned to face Frank. Frank pointed back toward me, signaling me to go first. From the crap she'd pulled that morning, I wanted to give her the gift of a towel. However, with a small amount of reservation and a disgruntled demeanor, I reached in the big pocket of my cargo shorts and handed her a watchcase. In the case was a Disney World watch she'd asked for last year when we went there for vacation. It was a teal color, with glow-in-the-dark hands shaped as hearts. Although she said she was thankful and gave me a hug, I could tell from her reaction that she was still bothered by the unaddressed issues we were having. Since the watch didn't bring her back around, I knew it would come down to a conversation, which I was ready to have. I just needed to find the right time to do it.

When Teresa saw the watch, her face scrunched up. "Em, y'all been married for almost five years, and that's all you get is a Disney watch? Girl, that couldn't be me."

I mugged back at Teresa, "And it will never be you! You ol' man-hatin' heathen. I'm surprised you still got something to say after that bull crap you pulled last night!"

Teresa rolled her eyes and frowned her face toward me. "Bshh, boy please. You ain't seen nothing. Tiff, you better get your man. He don't know who he talking to."

I raised my voice: "Oh, I know exactly who the hell I'm talking to…"

Tiffany screamed, "Enough already! Can y'all please cut it out! It's Christmas!" She lowered her voice to say, "Like I said earlier, Stu, I'm thankful for the watch, and I love it. Teresa, this is a great gift because he remembered something I said over a year ago. Then he took the time and effort to go find it for me. That shows that he cares and put a lot of thought into it. To me, that's priceless."

I nodded and said, "You're welcome babe," before Tiff gave me a hug.

Teresa smacked her lips. "Em, if you say so."

Once things had settled down a bit, I'd never seen Frank so bubbly. He looked toward Angel. "Angel, I know this Christmas hasn't been what you thought it was going to be, but have no fear, your granddad is here." Frank took a set of keys out of his pocket and tossed them to Angel with a smile on his face. "Tell me what they say baby girl," Frank requested in an arrogant tone.

Angel answered while holding the keys up to her face, "Um… gym locker…gun safe…storage unit…"

Frank stopped her. "Whoa, wait a minute, I gave you the wrong set." After getting his keys back, Frank handed Angel another set of keys. "Here you go. Now, what do they say?"

Angel's eyes looked like they were going to pop out of her head as she screamed, "BMW! Oh my gosh! Thank you so much Granddaddy!"

Frank replied, "You're welcome baby. It's a fully loaded, brand-new 2015 model too. Come on, let's go outside and take a look at it."

I hated to be the bearer of bad news, but I had to. I didn't want to set up Angel to have her feelings hurt even more. I blocked them from leaving the living room and told Frank as humbly as possible, "I don't know if you know this or not, but I'm sorry to tell you, Angel is only fifteen."

Tiffany chimed in, "Yeah Dad, she doesn't even have a learner's permit yet."

I finished with, "Yeah Mr. Frank, you don't want a car like that just sitting."

Frank questioned, "Well, I guess I'm just gonna have to drive it until you're ready for it, huh Angel?"

Angel, Tiffany, and I all said in unison, "Yeah, I guess so."

Now with all the gifts open, it was nearing midday. All the lights in the main living area were off, as the sunlight coming through the large windows provided plenty of interior illumination. I was sitting on the couch, directly beneath the ceiling fan, when Frank stood up and said that he was going to take a nap because he'd had a late night and early morning. George slowly stood up in agreement. "Yeah, I think I'ma get me a nap too. I'm sleepy as a narcoleptic working night shift."

I chuckled a bit as they both walked away. I was watching SportsCenter while Nancy, Tiffany, Teresa, and Angel picked up the wrapping paper on the floor, prior to them heading to Nancy's room. Even though I didn't think I was tired, eventually I dozed off on the couch.

———

The time was now about four o'clock. I was awakened by the vibration of my phone in my pocket. After looking at it, I saw that I had a text from Uncle Al. He was supposed to be coming over for dinner but informed me that he wasn't going to be able to make it because something came up. I texted him back to ask if everything was alright. All he replied back with was, "Yeah."

With exception of the diminishing natural sunlight, the appearance of the living area hadn't changed much. The recessed lighting in the kitchen was now being utilized by the women, who were in there cackling from amusement. I joined Tiffany and Angel at the bar to see what was so funny, as we all watched Nancy cook.

Nancy giggled as she said, "Hey Stuart, I was just in here telling Angel what her mama used to be like when she was fifteen." I was excited to hear this, then I realized Teresa wasn't there. After I asked, Angel told me that she was still asleep upstairs.

I couldn't wait because I knew this story was going to be good. Suddenly, Angel's phone rang, which stopped Nancy before she could even start. It was Roosevelt, Angel's dad, calling to tell her Merry Christmas. Angel put him on speakerphone so that we could all tell him Merry Christmas as well. Angel went on to tell her dad about her gifts and how she'd almost gotten a new car. Surprisingly, Roosevelt said, "Well Angel, I believe you *should* work for your first car baby. I mean, if you think about it, God intended for us to work. Why do you think Jesus was born with a manager?"

Nancy, Tiffany, Angel, and I silently cut our eyes at one another in confusion, as we turned our ears toward the phone to listen for clarity. I think our response of sheer quietness made him feel like he needed to explain further. As Roosevelt began to speak, Angel placed her phone on the countertop. "Yeah, that's right. Mary and Joseph were looking all over Bethlehem, trying to find a job for Jesus. Then they finally saw that they were hiring at the inn. So they walked in there and gave birth to lil baby Jesus. Then they wrapped him up in swaddled clothes and laid him in his manager's hands."

Nancy spoke up. "Hey Roosevelt, I think you're mistaking 'manager' for 'manger.'"

"You sure about that Ms. Nancy?" Roosevelt questioned.

"Yes baby, I'm sure," Nancy answered.

Roosevelt finished, "You know you might be right about that Ms. Nancy. My Sunday school teacher did have a lisp."

Nearly off the phone, with Tiffany and I in tears from laughing, Nancy said, "It's OK Roosevelt, just make sure you don't tell nobody else that story, alright?" Roosevelt agreed prior to hanging up.

Soon after, Tiffany told Angel to go upstairs to Nancy's room and get ready for dinner. Tiffany and I sat at the bar, not even turning to glance at each other. We both looked straight ahead at Nancy, who was running around the kitchen, cooking and complaining about how Frank doesn't clean up after himself when he cooks. Slowly, Nancy stood up after getting a pot from underneath the cabinet, then peeked over at us out of the corner of her eye. She tightened her jaws and tilted her head to the side in disappointment before turning to face us and leaning over the countertop with both hands on it.

"Listen to me. I know tension when I see it." She used her index finger to point at both of us individually before saying, "Both of you need to learn how to communicate with each other effectively. Don't let whatever crap you're going through now build up into something bigger. Y'all don't want to end up like Frank and me. It might seem funny, but it's miserable and lonely walking past someone every day like they're not even there." I couldn't believe Nancy read us that easily. What she had said definitely grabbed my attention though. She faced Tiffany to say, "Now Tiff, you're not perfect, and you're not going to find somebody perfect. Nor can you change Stuart into Mr. Perfect, so stop trying. You better learn how to love that man for who he is."

Nancy turned to face me before Tiffany spoke up. "Yeah, but he—"

Nancy cut her off by raising her voice. "It doesn't matter what he did!" That put a smile on my face as I looked toward Tiffany, who rolled her eyes at me. Nancy resumed, "Real love keeps no record of wrongdoing. Just think about it like this Tiff. When you met him, he didn't have a neck, but you married him anyway, didn't you?"

Tiffany giggled and nodded her head. My jaw dropped to the floor as I faced Nancy in shock. "Huh?"

"Boy hush," Nancy replied. "You know you ain't have no neck. Every time you'd nod your head, you gave your chin a chest bump." I didn't find that to be funny at all. I'll just say that Tiffany didn't feel the same way. With her focus back on Tiffany, Nancy advised, "Now, you can keep holding a grudge and not giving that man sex if you want to, but you ain't gonna be doing nothing but driving him away. Most of the time, it's away to another woman."

Tiffany's laughter had come to a complete stop as she and I didn't flinch, giving her mother our undivided attention. Nancy went on, "I'm not going to sit up here and act like I'm perfect, because I'm not. I shouldn't have taken that money and started that business without asking my husband first. I should've listened to my husband and let him be the leader that he is. Even with all that, it still doesn't give him the right to disrespect me and say all those demeaning things about me. That's why I filed for divorce, not because I didn't love him anymore."

Curiously, Tiffany inquired, "I always wondered: What attracted you to him in the first place Mama?"

Nancy took a deep breath as a slight grin came on her face. "You know your daddy blacker than fried chicken and grape soda. He wasn't any different back then either, except he had muscles from playing all those sports. He used to have all those abs with that black skin. Em, his stomach looked like burnt biscuits." Even Nancy laughed with us on that one before she went on. "See Tiff, I know what you're thinking. 'Yeah, but Ma, Daddy's 'bout as simple as a drowning fish.' Guess what? You're right. I know he's dumb enough to text me looking for his cell phone. But I love him, and he's always taken good care of me, even after our divorce." Tiffany rolled her eyes and slightly shook her head sideways as she blew out through her nose in frustration. Nancy explained, "If you're smart Tiffany, you'll listen to what I'm trying to tell you. See, nobody told me nothing about being a good wife until it was too late. All my mom ever told me was to keep his belly full and his penis down."

There was a moment of silence as Nancy looked us both in the eyes individually. I wanted to tell Nancy that it sounded like she and Frank felt the same way about each other. They just needed to figure out a way to treat one another and let go of the past. I didn't say anything though. I figured: Who am I to speak? Even after the advice I'd received from Nancy, Frank, and George, I still wasn't on good terms with my wife.

Since I'd agreed with most everything Nancy had said, with the exception of my neck, I spoke with a grin to break the silence. "Yeah Ma, I was going to ask you about that. How is it that you eat so healthy but then go and open a Fish Fry and Yoga Studio?"

Nancy said, "Oh, just because I don't eat it don't mean I can't cook it." Then she warmed up a piece for me out of the refrigerator. That fish tasted so good that I thought she had a legit business idea too.

Of course, Tiffany still wasn't speaking to me, but she was nibbling off my plate. In frustration, with my head tilted, I asked, "Hey Ma, what did you say Tiffany was like when she was fifteen?" Tiffany didn't like that I brought that back up, but I didn't care.

By now, Nancy had her back turned to us with two pans in the oven and a large pot of vegetables on the stove. She spoke with enthusiasm. "Oh yeah, I forgot. She wanted to be an international businesswoman. So she found this brown leather suitcase with matching strap at some thrift store and used that as her book bag. Then she put a bunch of stickers of other countries' flags on it and took it everywhere she went. People thought she was a straight A student, when really, her grades were so bad she couldn't pass a survey." I chuckled before Nancy continued, "But she picked them up in college though. Then, after college, before she met you, she went through her lil phase of unemployed men."

Tiffany almost choked on a fish bone trying to cut her mom off. After we gave her some white bread and Kool-Aid, Tiffany defended herself. "Don't say that Ma. That's not true. Every man I dated had a job."

Nancy questioned Tiffany: "Oh yeah? Which one?"

I sat at the edge of the stool to hear this. Tiffany said, "Well what about Travis? He was a pharmaceutical representative."

"No, he sold drugs," Nancy replied. "That's why he is in jail now. Illegal jobs don't count."

Tiffany pleaded, "OK, well Dante. He sold food stamps. That's not illegal."

I thought to myself: *I guess common sense ain't common.* I looked over at Nancy, who appeared to be thinking the same thing, before I told Tiffany, "Um, yeah, that is illegal Tiff."

Tiffany responded, "I didn't know that was illegal. My dad used to buy food stamps from him all the time."

Nancy spoke up. "I already told you earlier that your daddy dumb enough to go to the library looking for a Facebook. Besides, Stuart doesn't need to hear all our business. Focus on your unemployed past."

Tiffany smacked her lips at her mom, then she said, "OK, Eric. He was in the military."

Nancy rolled her eyes in the sky, but I took a sigh of relief. "Whew, now we're talking. What branch was he in?"

Tiffany looked at me, confused. "I don't know. I think it was just him and his cousins."

I told her, "No. There has to be a branch. The military is huge. You know, like army, navy, marines, et cetera."

Tiffany explained, "Oh, no. I think you misunderstood me. I meant Da Military. They were an R&B group that he played the drums for. They did a pretty good job selling their demos in the mall for a while too."

Nancy didn't even acknowledge her; she just turned around and finished cooking.

I stood up to say, "What the hell?"

Tiffany couldn't believe I didn't know who they were. "What's wrong Stu? You don't remember them? On their album cover it was a picture of all of them wearing a piece of their stepdaddy's uniform."

I'd had enough. "Tiffany that isn't a real job."

Tiffany argued, "Yes it is. They sold CDs, and had hits too."

Hoping that maybe she would name some songs to jog my memory and bring some legitimacy to her argument, I asked, "What hits did they have?"

Tiffany grabbed her chin and looked down at the bar. "Um, let's see. They had a couple that everybody liked. Oh, 'Don't Eat

My Fries 'Cause They're in the Same Bag As Yours' and 'Brushing for Waves.' Then they had, 'Stop Rolling Up the Toothpaste.' That one was probably their best song. It got some radio play." I just ignored her like Nancy did and walked upstairs to get ready for dinner.

CHAPTER 5

Test Driving

The time was now 5:30 p.m. I stood between the bed and the entry door in a bedroom, wearing only my boxers. I was in the process of changing clothes for dinner. As I was attempting to grab my jeans and polo out of my duffel bag, Tiffany walked in and quickly closed the door behind her. Caught off guard, I said, "Hey—"

She put her index finger over her lips—"Shhh"—then pushed me on the bed. Usually, I'm not into all that dominatrix stuff. But hell, by that point I was willing to take it however I could get it.

After we made sweet, passionate love, the time was now 5:33 p.m. While lying side by side, we looked into each other's eyes. I was breathing rather hard, while Tiffany was as calm as a summer's breeze. She appeared to have been disappointed with our recent intimacy. I figured now was a better time than ever to say, "Tiffany, I'm so sorry about everything. I could argue, but it would be pointless. All I care about is you and making sure that we are on the same page."

She reached to hold my hand. "No, it's not all your fault. I owe you an apology too. I feel like everything could have been avoided had I communicated with you up front, especially with the things dealing with Angel." Our conversation went on for a short while as we discussed ways to prevent this from happening in the future.

Toward the end of our discussion, the doorbell rang. While getting dressed, I could hear Frank and George answering the door. I couldn't make out the other voices though, and there was no need to. Tiffany got excited while jumping into her jeans. "Oh, that's my aunt Sabrina." I was anxious to meet her too because I'd heard so much about her. It also made me wonder where Uncle Al was if Sabrina was here. I decided to stay out of his business though, and just go eat dinner.

Tiffany and I walked out of the room overlooking a fully lit living area and kitchen. The darkness of the night had blackened the windows in the living room, where there was an iPod dock playing Ray Charles's version of "Baby, It's Cold Outside." We were halfway down the stairs, and the overwhelming smell of the food had my appetite growing by the second. That's when I was able to see Sabrina and her date standing in the foyer, along with Teresa, Nancy, and Angel.

I could finally confirm that all the rumors were true. Sabrina looked better than a sign that said, "FREE GAS." She stood about five foot nine in her open-toed stilettos, wearing khaki-colored capris and a low-cut blouse, all of which put her overly feminine physique on display. After Tiffany introduced us, Sabrina opened her arms for a hug. She was in great shape too. When I hugged her, her body felt better than good credit. Along with a picture-perfect smile surrounded by red lipstick, Sabrina's dimples caused a ruffle in her otherwise flawless, radiant, oak-toned skin. "Hi, I'm Stuart. It's nice to finally meet you."

While tucking her straight, long, jet-black hair behind her ears, which uncovered a beige hearing aid, she replied, "It's nice to meet you too." Sabrina then turned to face her date while saying, "And this is my boyfriend, Henry." Henry looked exactly like Uncle Al had described him. If he'd cut that thick goatee off his face, he would definitely look like Emmanuel Lewis. Henry made me feel uneasy around him though. He held a bulky, white, living room table Bible in his right hand, with his chin held high, while rocking back and forth on the balls of his feet. The first thing that crossed my mind was that he had a Napoleon complex. The second thing to cross my mind was that I didn't want to feel like I was sitting through Bible study during grace. I reserve those prayers for my aunt Belle.

When Henry spoke in a clear, masculine tone, he did nothing but confirm my assumptions. "Happy Holidays, Mr. and Mrs. Jones. Pleased to make your acquaintance." I was thinking to myself: *Where was Shane when I needed him?*

In an attempt to be hospitable, Tiffany replied with formal dialect: "We're pleased to make your acquaintance as well Mr. Henry."

Henry then turned to face me. I had to bend over to reach his little raccoon hand, but when I did, I just gave him a fist bump. Then I told him, "Stay black." My brother Shane would've been proud, but Tiffany rolled her eyes in disappointment.

Sabrina and Nancy didn't hear what I had said because they had begun their own conversation. Plus, with the noise of everyone conversing in the kitchen as Frank and George set the table, nobody heard me. It was then though, that I found out Sabrina and Nancy were talking about me. After Nancy told her that I was Tammy's nephew, Sabrina went on a long rant. "Oh, you're Tammy's nephew? Em. I can't stand that heffa. She can't keep a man without lying to him. You know I had to beat her down, don't you?"

I was about to express how I couldn't have cared less about that whole situation. Before I was able to speak though, Tiffany spoke up. "Dang Aunt Sabrina, you sound like you're still bitter."

She quickly responded, "Yeah that's right, I hit her." Henry reached up to rub Sabrina's lower back for soothing comfort.

Nancy raised her voice. "No, she said you sound bitter!"

Sabrina started getting pissed. "I already told you I hit her! How many times you want me to say it?" Then she looked down at her boyfriend, Henry, who was signaling her to turn up the volume on her hearing aid. She responded to him with, "Oh, OK," while adjusting her earpiece, followed by asking, "Now what you say about me and Tammy?"

Everybody was so tired of yelling at that point, Nancy just waved her off. "Nothing Sabrina. You hit her, you hit her."

Soon after, we were all gathered in the dining room and kitchen. Frank had inserted the leaf in the table so that it could seat eight. I sat with my back against the wall, facing the living room, with Tiffany to my left and George's designated seat to my right. Nancy sat with her back to the kitchen, at the end of the table, while Frank sat at the other end of the table. Currently, the only person sitting across from me was Sabrina, who sat in the middle seat. We were still waiting on George, Henry, Teresa, and Angel to finish making their plates.

I kept my eyes on Henry as he walked toward the table with that huge Bible still in his right hand and his plate in the other hand. Once he got to his seat, he put his plate on the table. Then quickly, as if it were all one motion, he put the Bible in the chair and jumped to sit on top of it. After Henry nudged Sabrina, she didn't even turn away from the conversation she was having with Nancy to scoot him up closer to the table. I started looking around to see if anyone else had seen what I just saw. I guess they were all too busy in their own conversations to notice. I was still in shock though, not only because he was a grown man using the Bible like a kid uses the telephone book, but also because he and Sabrina did it so smooth. It was like they were partners, working together to overcome short-people problems.

Henry had begun to organize his silverware when George grabbed everyone's attention with his elevated voice. "Where's the ham!"

Still sitting, Nancy looked over her shoulder while cutting her eyes at George. "You know I don't cook no pork Mr. George."

George countered with, "Yeah, but it's Christmas. On Thanksgiving, you're supposed to have turkey. On New Year's, you're supposed to have black-eyed peas." His voice gradually amplified as he spoke. "And on Christmas, you're supposed to have *ham*!"

Sabrina playfully slapped Nancy on the shoulder. "Whoo, girl it's been a long time since I've had a Spam sandwich."

Tiffany butted in. "He didn't say Spam Aunt Sabrina, he said *ham*!"

Sabrina sat back in her chair. "Oh, Nancy I thought you told me you stopped cooking pork."

No one responded to her. We all just shook our heads before Frank suggested, "Hey Dad, just look at it this way. Baby Jesus didn't have ham when he was born."

George explained, "Yeah, that's because he had one wise man and two dummies." I had to force myself not to giggle so I could hear him finish. George continued, "Think about it. They gave gold, frankincense, and myrrh. Which ain't nothing but money, incense, and perfume. I can understand the gold, because you need money when you have a baby. But in my opinion, they would've had at least two wise men had one of them brought some ham. They know that baby needed to eat. Besides, who was the biblical pediatrician anyway? They had lil baby Jesus covered in perfume, laying in a room full of incense." Tiffany and I were leaning on each other, laughing hysterically.

Sabrina got up and started gathering her things as if she were about to leave. Teresa asked from the kitchen, "Where are you going Aunt Sabrina? You just got here."

Sabrina started waving her index finger around. "Look, I'm sorry, but I don't want no bugs in my house. I'll come back over once y'all get rid of these insects."

George slapped his hand down hard on the countertop. "I said INCENSE! Lord have mercy! You might be fine, but you deaf as a motherfucka!"

Henry stood on top of his Bible to defend Sabrina. "*Excuse me! I believe our vernacular is extensive enough for us to speak on a much higher plane than the one we have been communicating on thus far.*" I didn't know if I should be offended or not. From the way everyone was looking around at one another, confused and in silence, I figured I was not alone. I decided to take Tiffany's lead on that one; she seemed to understand him the best.

Without warning, the doorbell rang, breaking up the tension in the dining room. I looked down at my phone to see that it was 6:00 p.m. on the dot. Sabrina, Henry, and George sat back down at the table, while Frank got up to answer the door.

I couldn't believe it. It was Chris and Brittany...together. Sabrina got back up to greet her son with a hug. Nancy left the table to console Teresa at the bar with a shoulder rub. "It's OK baby, we will get through this together."

Teresa pulled away from her mom and looked up at her, puzzled. "Get through what Ma? I keep telling y'all we just friends. I knew she had a boyfriend. I just didn't know it was Klepto. I mean Chris. Besides, I'm strictly dickly anyway."

Frank was thinking the same thing I was thinking when he asked, "So Brittany, you mean to tell me you're not...uh?" He cut himself off by saying, "Aw hell, never mind. Merry Christmas. Can I take your jacket?"

After Frank took her jacket to hang, I noticed Brittany had changed her appearance as well. She had straightened her sandy-blond hair and wore a spaghetti-strapped, baby-blue dress with flowers on it. She even managed to squeeze those husky tenders into some high-heel shoes. Chris, being "The Reelist," wore a white T-shirt, denim jeans, and Nike boots. Brittany spoke as she approached the table. "Hey everyone. I can tell by you all's faces that you are just as shocked as I was twenty minutes ago. When I told Chris where we were going, he said that was his family."

Chris extended both of his arms out to the side and shouted with a grin, "And now we here!"

Frank went to grab a foldout chair from the garage for Chris to sit in. Sabrina helped Henry scoot down so Chris could sit beside Nancy at the head of the table, and Brittany sat between Chris and Sabrina. Teresa and Angel saw the seating was full and decided to sit at the bar. While Nancy was up, she made Chris's and Brittany's plates.

Now that Brittany was standing closer to me, I was able to see that she still had her masculine features. Her broad shoulders and ripped-up chest stretched those spaghetti straps to their limit. She had a V-neck farmer's tan too, that made her body look whiter than an ashy albino. George said, "You look lovely Ms. Brittany."

As she replied with a thank you, my eyes popped open. I almost broke my neck turning to stare at George. I started wondering if it was the eye doctor that I had picked him up from the day before.

Once seated, Frank asked Chris to bless the food since this was his first Christmas with the family in some years. Chris seemed hesitant to do it, so Brittany used her large hands to rub his back for encouragement. Frank said, "All heads bowed and eyes closed." Before I closed my eyes, I saw Brittany yank her hand off Chris's back because her calluses had gotten stuck to the back of his T-shirt.

Chris questioned Frank, "You sure about that Unc?"

"Absolutely Chris," Nancy answered. "We're so glad you're home. I think that's a great idea."

Frank, George, Sabrina, and I all nodded our heads in concurrence before Chris responded, "Thanks Aunt Nancy. I appreciate that." Then that big smile of his came back. "But Uncle Frank, I'm not nervous about saying the prayer. I was asking: Are you sure that everyone will have their eyes closed?"

I looked straight up at the ceiling to keep from laughing. Frank replied, "You know what Klepto, since I saw how you got a lil excited about the thought of everyone's eyes being closed, everybody else can bow their heads and close their eyes. I'm keeping my eyes open and on you."

The smile left Chris's face as he began to pray:

"Lord, thank you for this food that we are about to receive, without the guards looking over our shoulders saying, 'Hurry up inmate. Naptime in twenty minutes!' Thank you for the real silverware and not the rewashed plastic utensils. It took me five minutes to cut through my chicken breasts. Lord thank you for blessing us with leftovers. Now we don't have to worry about Big Terrence coming around asking for other people's food. No Big Terrence! I said you should ask for a second plate! I don't want to be your second mate!"

I was caught off guard by that one, so naturally I shouted, "Hey man! I mean, amen. Amen."

Chris apologized. "I'm sorry. I had a lil flashback." Nancy and Brittany rubbed his back while telling him it was OK. George and Frank squinted their eyes and shook their heads in disbelief.

Tiffany wasn't bothered by the prayer. "Wow Chris, it's still crazy to me that I haven't seen you in so long."

Chris agreed. "Yeah, the last time I saw you, Angel was a little girl, and you were dating her dad. No offense Stuart." I told him there was no offense taken. Chris never came off to me as the disrespectful type. Tiffany smacked her lips and grunted, which made Chris ask, "So what happened to y'all, anyway?" Tiffany and I rarely ever talk about our pasts, so I was anxious to hear too.

Tiffany pouted her lips and shrugged her shoulders. "He was just childish and had too many pet peeves. Roosevelt claims he broke up with me because my toes were too long."

I jumped in the conversation. "Well, you never know. Y'all were so young. That could've been a legitimate reason for him at the time."

Tiffany looked back at me. "Really Stu? My toes were too long? Come on now?"

I didn't want to tell her that I could see why Roosevelt did it. Tiffany's long, wrinkled-up toes made her look like she was walking on bacon strips. I decided to sugarcoat it for her. "You're right Tiff, that is immature. Most men wouldn't leave a woman over something like that. You must admit though, your toes are kinda long." Tiffany sat up in her seat. I put both my hands up. "Whoa, wait a minute Tiff. Your toes don't bother me. In fact, they come in handy sometimes. Remember when you used them to unbuckle my belt and unbutton my pants—"

Frank put his fist down on the table and yelled, "Hey hey hey! That's my daughter! Don't nobody want to hear all that at the dinner table!"

Chris was cheesing. "Shiiid, speak for yourself Unc. I just got out, and a good story goes a long way. Please Stuart…continue."

Brittany elbowed him in the arm as I shouted, "Klepto shut the hell up!"

Tiffany always liked hearing people's stories, so she asked, "Enough about us. Chris, how did you end up meeting Brittany?"

Brittany and Chris both looked at each other, giggling and play arguing, "No, you say it. No, you say it." I was getting so sick of them, if I knew the story, I would've said it. Chris explained, "So they had started the carpentry program at the prison, and I signed up. Brittany was the one who hand carried all the wood from the dump truck to the lumberyard. When she saw me through the fence, she said I was cute. So once I confirmed she was a woman, I told her to write me, and she did it. We started writing each other back and forth, and the rest is history."

Immediately following, Brittany sat up in her chair to cheerfully say, "At our church, we have this contest called 'Unique Love.' The way it works is, couples write down how they started dating, and whoever's story is chosen as the most unique wins a thousand dollars. Chris doesn't want to do it though. He doesn't think we will win."

All the women encouraged Chris to do it, while George and I had our eyes fully exposed with our heads down in disbelief of everything we had just heard. Frank spoke up to break the chatter. "Listen to me! If y'all don't win that thousand dollars, I will personally give my life to Christ, just so I can read the letter of the winners."

Teresa was over at the bar, eating and dropping crumbs on the floor because of her spacious teeth, before Henry offered, "I apologize Mr. Chris. I was not made aware of your previous dwelling. I have witnessed far too often the difficulties that are accompanied with post prison employment. As a friend of your mother and the owner of Henry's Heating and Air Conditioning, I would like to offer you a full-time position with benefits, starting next week if you are willing to accept."

I didn't understand everything he said, but I did hear that he owned his own HVAC company. The first thing that popped in my mind was that maybe he could fix all that extra air coming out of

Teresa's mouth. Frank mentioned, "Yeah Klepto, that would be the perfect job for you. You can't steal air."

Frank and most everyone else were pushing Chris to take the job. I couldn't focus though, because Henry had asked George to pass him the pepper. George did pass the pepper, but he placed it slightly beyond Henry's reach, toward the middle of the table. This really grabbed my attention when Henry reached for the pepper, then found out it was too far for his little alligator arms. He tried to fake by grabbing his glass like he was thirsty. With the combination of his partner in short crimes, Sabrina, not being able to reach it, and Henry's proud Napoleon mind-set refusing to ask for help, I knew Henry was upset.

Before too long, Chris decided to take Henry up on his offer. That was when Sabrina leaned back in her chair to look toward the bar. "So Teresa, are you seeing anybody right now?"

Teresa pulled her neck back and squeezed her eyebrows together. "Where is this coming from Aunt Sabrina?"

Sabrina quickly responded, "Wait a minute, calm down. I was just wondering because you're such a pretty young lady, and you have your own business. I just feel like you would have a lot to offer a young man who's looking to settle down and start a family."

Teresa put her fork down, and while still sitting, turned around to face the table as she shook her head. "I'm sorry Aunt Sabrina. I might be thirty-three, but I'm not desperate. I can't see myself settling with no man who thinks that he will have any say in what I do. Just look at Tiffany. She acts like she can't do nothing without talking to Stuart about it first." I could feel Tiffany's arm tighten as Teresa looked at me. "I'm not going to spend the rest of my life stroking some insecure-ass man's ego."

I was so angry I could feel my blood boiling as I quickly stood up to say thoughtlessly, "What! Shut your mouth, and your teeth, you snaggletooth skank!" Tiffany stood beside me as we watched everyone's eyes get big while they looked at me in shock. Still in rage, I yelled, "Don't look at me like that! Y'all know that girl's teeth messed up! Her mouth looks like it had more hits than The O'Jays." George laughed so hard he almost knocked me into Tiffany as he leaned against me.

Teresa stood up to say, "You not going to talk to me like that!"

I started talking over her. "I WILL TALK TO YOU HOWEVER THE HELL I WANT TO! That seems to be the only way your dumb ass understands. Got the nerve to call yourself a hairstylist, and ain't got a client or customer. Hell, your mama won't even let you touch her head." Nancy dropped her head like she was saying grace again. I finished by saying, "And I ain't insecure! Tiffany and I both talk to each other before we do things! It's called working together! That's what you do in a marriage. But you don't have to worry about that though! You're gonna be single for the rest of your life with that mouth of yours, and I'm not talking about your teeth this time either!"

Teresa rolled her eyes. "Tiffany you need to talk to your man 'cause he trippin' right now."

Tiffany explained, "No Teresa, you're the one that's trippin', and stop calling him my man. That's my husband, and there's no ego stroking going on around here. I don't get down like that, trust me. I listen to him and follow his lead because he is a good husband, and in every decision he always makes sure that Angel and I are taken care of first."

Teresa butted in, "Oh, so what about that time—"

Tiffany cut her off. "Hey! I said he was good, not perfect! One of the biggest mistakes I ever made when we first got married was calling you when we had arguments! You still want to bring up stuff that we've forgotten about!"

I felt such relief and joy having my wife back me up the way that she did. Everyone at the table had also calmed down at this point, but their attention was still fixated on Teresa and Tiffany. During the brief pause in their discussion, I managed to apologize to everyone, especially Angel, for my use of foul language earlier. After I received head nods and verbal acceptances, Tiffany switched gears. "Teresa, you are thirty-three years old, single, no kids, and never been married. When are you going to realize that it's not the men, it's you? I mean, think about it. Even your exceptionally strong best friend found a man." I wasn't sure if it was embarrassment, realization, the fact that those words came from her sister, or an accumulation of the three, but Teresa dropped her head in tears. We could all hear her crying as she ran upstairs to her room.

As soon as her door slammed shut, the entire house turned pitch black. I couldn't even see my hand in front of my face. I heard George's chair scoot back beside me as he spoke, "I'm going to go reset the panel box next to my room."

George used his cell phone to see, while Frank banged his fist on the table again. "That daggone mouse must be eating through the electrical lines!"

"What's that jingling sound I keep hearing?" Sabrina asked.

Nancy was so afraid she became irritated. "Sabrina hush. You couldn't hear gunshots in a western."

Chris cut in, "Shh. No. Listen, I hear it too."

"That's just Grandpa George's watch rattling again," Tiffany said nonchalantly.

George responded from the hallway, causing a slight echo. "I'm not wearing a watch, and I hear that jingling sound too. It sounds like it's near me."

Obviously annoyed, Angel raised her voice. "Come on you all. How many times do I have to say that I'm almost sixteen. I know there is no Santa Claus, so please stop with the games already."

I responded to her comment. "I really wish we were playing Angel. Unfortunately, right now we're not."

"Frank, if you don't get your hairy foot off of me! Now isn't the time to be playing footsie," Nancy demanded.

Frank replied, "Ain't nobody trying to play footsie with you Nancy. The last time I did that, I had to get stitches. Besides, how are my feet going to reach yours when I'm way on the other side of the table?"

Frank's comment made me do a quick process of elimination, as Nancy pulled out her phone to look. I knew it wasn't Henry's feet because they were dangling from the Bible chair. The only other person I could think of with hairy feet was Brittany, and from the way those thick ham hocks were stuffed in her high-heel shoes earlier, I figured she would just be happy sitting. Then I remembered Teresa dropping the crumbs and Solo saying that we would be able to hear the mouse's footsteps on the hardwood floor.

Before I had a chance to say anything, Nancy had already scooted her chair away from the table when the lights in the house came back on. Since she didn't need it anymore, Nancy placed her phone on the table as she leaned to the side to see what was on her feet.

"AHHH!" Nancy screamed in a screeching voice, then kicked her leg beneath the table. I looked under the table and saw that it was a dead mouse Nancy had just kicked off her feet. What made it worse though, was that Nancy was wearing thong ankle-strap sandals. So the dead mouse had been lying on her bare skin while the lights were out.

Still kicking her legs and shaking in disgust, Nancy forcefully shoved her chair away from the table even more to get up. As she did so, the chair tipped over backward with Nancy still in it, causing her to hit the back of her head on the countertop on her way down to the hardwood floors.

Tiffany screamed, "Mama!" Frank and George ran over to help Chris get her up. Nancy wasn't moving at all. I rushed to dial 911 on my phone. While the phone was ringing, Sabrina, Tiffany, and Angel were in tears as they yelled for Nancy to get back up. Henry had hopped out of his Bible chair, and without ducking his head, walked underneath the table to remove the mouse with a napkin and dustpan.

"911, what's your emergency?" a lady asked after picking up the phone.

Still worried, I said loudly, "We need an ambulance! My mother-in-law just hit her head on the countertop, and now she's laid out on the floor, not moving!"

The woman responded, "OK sir, I need you to tell me if she still has a pulse."

After I asked Frank, he told me that she did have a pulse. I answered the woman, "Yes."

She exhaled. "Whew. OK, that's great news sir. She will still need to be brought in to regain consciousness, and for testing to ensure her overall health from this incident. Unfortunately though sir, due to the holiday, we are short staffed on ambulance drivers, and all of them are currently out on calls. I would highly recommend that you bring her to the emergency room yourself as opposed to waiting for the next available driver."

I hung up the phone and then said to everyone, "We're gonna have to take her ourselves."

"What did they say?" Henry asked.

I paused for a second; I was shocked to hear him sound regular for once. "They're short staffed on ambulance drivers because it's Christmas Day, and all the drivers they *do* have are already out on calls."

Brittany grabbed her keys and jacket. "We can take my truck since I'm blocking everybody in." She then ran outside.

Frank started feeling around in his pockets. "Wait a minute. Before we pick her up off the floor, let me make sure I have my insurance card in my wallet."

Chris had his back turned to everyone with his head down before he spoke up. "Yeah, it's in there Unc, right beside the losing lottery tickets."

Frank shouted, "Give me my got damn wallet Klepto!" Then he snatched his wallet out of Chris's hands as he continued to speak. "Now come over here and help me pick your aunt up. You too Stuart. She ain't as petite as she used to be."

We were almost at the foyer with Nancy when Brittany busted through the front door. "Lay her on the couch! My truck won't start!" While everyone grunted and smacked their lips, prior to talking about different options, I called the only person I knew who could find a way to drive over on Christmas Day: my Uncle Al.

Uncle Al answered the phone. "What's going on Nephew?"

In a rush, I spoke fast and abruptly. "You busy right now?"

Uncle Al said nonchalantly, "No, right now I'm not, but in about fifteen minutes or so I will be."

I curiously asked, "What's happening in fifteen minutes?"

Uncle Al explained, "Well, they say if you got an erection lasting longer than four hours, you need to call somebody. I got about fifteen minutes to go. The only reason I took that pill was because Sabrina told me she would meet me over here."

I shook my head as I looked up at Sabrina. "Never mind all that Unc! Nancy banged her head on the countertop, and now she's out cold. We tried calling 911, but there are no more ambulances available. Now Brittany's truck is blocking the driveway, and it won't start. Can you come take Nancy to the hospital?"

Uncle Al's voice perked up. "What! Aw man! Yeah I'ma need to find something to drive, but I'll be there by eight o'clock."

Before I could even say good-bye, he had already hung up the phone. I looked down at my phone and saw that the time now was 7:40 p.m. Any other time, I would've questioned my Uncle Al's thought process because I didn't see how he was going to be able to find a vehicle to drive and make it over to the house in twenty minutes. However, given the situation we were in, I decided to let Uncle Al do his thing.

With the exception of Brittany and Frank, everyone else stood in the living room, over top of Nancy, fanning her with whatever they could find to use. I grabbed everyone's attention. "My Uncle Al is on his way. He said he should be here in twenty minutes."

Most everyone took a sigh of relief, except for Sabrina. "Who did you say?"

I repeated myself. "Uncle Al."

Sabrina rolled her eyes and smacked her lips.

Subsequently, Tiffany had thought about what I said and asked, "Wait a minute. Does Al even have a car?"

I didn't want everyone to lose hope, and my Uncle Al had never not kept his word, so I lied, "He told me he had a car." Immediately, I walked out of the front door to avoid any more questions and to let Frank and Brittany know.

Instantly, I felt the change in climate from the well-ventilated interior to the muggy heat of the dark, star-filled evening. I walked over to Brittany's four-by-four pickup truck with a lift kit, parked horizontally at the end of the driveway. The hood was raised, with Frank and Brittany bent over looking underneath it.

"Uncle Al said he should be here by eight o'clock," I said.

Frank and Brittany stood up to look at me as they both wiped their hands off with spare towels. Frank then looked down at his watch. "Oh, that's good."

Brittany questioned, "I thought he rode with you Stuart?"

Frank turned to face Brittany as he answered for me. "That don't mean nothing when it comes to his Uncle Al. That man will test-drive anything." Frank turned to face me before he finished. "Except maybe that shiny piece of shit you got parked in my driveway Stuart."

Brittany giggled, and I pouted my lips to ignore him. "Whatever. Were y'all able to fix the problem?"

Brittany replied, "No. The battery and the alternator both look good, so we're thinking that it's the starter. I just got off the phone with my buddy, who is a mechanic. He said he would be able to have it replaced for me in about an hour or so."

Frank cut in, "Yeah, we were lucky that her friend had the part she needed laying around at his shop."

I nodded in agreement.

Without warning, I heard loud sirens. Then I saw bright lights coming toward us at the end of the cul-de-sac, with a faint fluttering sound in the distance. It was so dark that I couldn't tell if it was an ambulance or a police car. I assumed it was an ambulance though, since I had called for one earlier. I was wrong. As the vehicle got closer and began to park in front of Frank's house, I was able to see that it was a police car with a Cessna 172 behind it.

Uncle Al hopped out of that little plane, yelling in our direction, "Come on y'all! Where's Nancy at?! We need to go!" I had never been happier to see my Uncle Al. I looked down at my watch, which showed that he had made it with three minutes to spare at 7:57 p.m.

As Frank, Uncle Al, and I ran into the house, with Uncle Al's erection leading the way, I asked, "Uncle Al, how did you manage to drive a personal airplane?"

Uncle Al answered, "That's one of the perks of being an airline mechanic. You get to park the smaller aircrafts. So I just grabbed one and drove it over here. That cop stopped me on the way, and I told him I was just taking it for a test-drive. He didn't believe me though. So I told him about everything we had goin' on, and then he decided to give me an escort over here."

Fortunately, Sabrina was in the restroom when we rushed in to grab Nancy. I didn't want Uncle Al to lose focus. We also couldn't find Chris to help us lift Nancy. After I asked, Angel told us that he was upstairs in the bathroom—the police sirens made him piss his pants.

Once on the porch, we noticed the cop standing in the street beside the cruiser, waving us over. According to the officer, not only did he have to use his car to take us, but Uncle Al was not to leave his sight until the Cessna 172 was returned safe and sound.

Tiffany wanted to go, but Frank insisted that I come instead to help with the lifting. I gave Tiffany a kiss on the forehead and told her everything would be fine. Then I got in the back seat of the police car with Nancy between Uncle Al and me. Frank sat up front with the police officer. My head slammed back into the seat as we scurried away.

CHAPTER 6

My Gift

The tires screeched and slid before coming to a complete stop in front of the emergency room at 8:15 p.m. After grabbing Nancy, we raced through the outdoor entryway, which was laced with bugs attracted to the illumination. The officer held the door open for us, then yelled for a doctor. As a nurse hurried toward us with a stretcher, I took that time to look around. Like most hospitals, it appeared to be overly sterile and bland, with an excess of room-dominating, bright lights. The scarce amount of people in the lobby seemed to all be sitting in one area, bobbing their heads and mumbling along to "The Mistletoe Jam" by Luther Vandross, which played on the speakers above.

As the officer ran back out to move his car, we gently placed Nancy on the stretcher and began pushing her down the hallway as fast as we could. The nurse led the way while asking questions about what had happened so that she could explain it to the doctor when he arrived. Frank did all the talking since he was directly behind the nurse on Nancy's left-hand side. I helped guide the stretcher on Nancy's right-hand side, while Uncle Al pushed from the back, leaning over Nancy's head.

With the hallway lights passing over us, I looked down to see if Nancy had regained consciousness from all the movement that had taken place. That's when I noticed the bulge in Uncle Al's pants bumping her in the forehead with every step he took. As we arrived at her room, I silently tried to grab Uncle Al's attention to get him to stop. It was too late though. Frank noticed what was going on and shouted, "Al, what the hell you doing?!"

Uncle Al looked down and then stepped back in shock. "Oh man! My bad Frank. I can't feel nothing with these pills."

Surprisingly, we didn't have to wait at all. The doctor rushed in the room, asking the nurse, "Has the patient regained consciousness at all?"

Still looking at Uncle Al, Frank spoke for her. "Well if she did, she lost it on the stretcher!" With his hands on his hips, Uncle Al turned his head and blew out hard through his nostrils in discouragement. He then followed me out into the hallway. Frank stayed in the room and closed the door behind us.

Once in the hallway, I checked my phone for the time, which was 8:30 p.m. That's when I noticed Tiffany had sent me a text asking what room her mother was in. Before I could respond, I heard Tiffany's voice call my name. I looked up, and she was running toward me from about twenty yards away, with Sabrina not too far behind. I could also see Henry walking in our direction at a normal pace, farther back.

Tiffany greeted me with a firm hug after running face first into my chest with tears in her eyes. I nestled her in my arms as I leaned over to give her a kiss on the cheek before asking, "How did you guys get here?" Tiffany said that when Brittany's friend showed up to fix her truck, he was nice enough to give them a ride over before he started. I nodded my head as I said, "That was nice of him. Oh, and I'm sorry for not responding to your text. I literally just saw it."

Tiffany replied, "It's OK. The lady at the front desk told me the room number."

We said, "I love you," to each other, and Tiffany gathered herself emotionally prior to walking in the room and closing the door behind her.

Without warning, Uncle Al busted out, "Emmm em! Sabrina! Sabrina! Sabrina! Girl, the last time I seen something that looked as good as you, it came with a side of fries!" Uncle Al stretched out his arms to finish. "Girl come here and show me some love."

Sabrina, who was teary-eyed like Tiffany, requested sharply, "Get out my face Al!" Henry had also walked up by this time and stood beside Sabrina. He reached up and rubbed the back of her thigh to comfort her in her time of need. I don't know if it was Sabrina's rejection, seeing Henry with Sabrina, or both. But in that moment, Uncle Al's erection disappeared.

Uncle Al questioned Sabrina's hostility toward him. "What's all the attitude for baby?"

Sabrina answered, "Attitude? You should've got the hint when I wasn't at my house, and I didn't show up at the hotel."

Uncle Al cut in. "Yeah, I was going to ask you about that."

Sabrina replied, "I was hoping you would catch a beatdown from my boyfriend when you came to my house. After I found out you didn't though, because you lied about who you were, I decided to keep you out of my Christmas dinner by keeping you in your hotel room."

I was leaning against the wall with my thumbs dipped in my pockets, not wanting anything to do with this conversation. Henry looked up at Sabrina with squinted eyes, asking, "Wait a second sweetheart. Do you mean to tell me that he is not a friend of the family?"

Without thought, Sabrina answered with an agitated tone, "No he ain't no friend of the family! That's Chris's dad, Al."

Henry stared at Al with his face squeezed together in anger. "Oh, so you were the one who kept switching jobs to avoid child support, back in a day?"

After snapping his head back in shock, Uncle Al quickly responded, "Whoa! Hold up now short stack. I was fired from all my jobs. I would never quit for some child support."

I felt like I needed to speak up for Uncle Al on this one, so I butted in. "Now that's true. I can vouch that my Uncle Al can't keep a job."

Uncle Al slowly turned to face me while scratching his head. "I don't know how I feel about that Stu, but thank you...I guess."

I got off the wall to give him a pat on the back. "No problem Unc. Anytime."

Henry was still outraged as he took a step toward Uncle Al. "Either way, I can't believe you showed up to my house and knocked on my door! I know you saw my boots on the front step."

Uncle Al raised his right hand to explain. "First of all, I didn't know that was your house, and I apologize for that. But if you talking about those lil G.I. Joe boots I saw, I figured Sabrina might be babysitting somebody."

Henry clapped slowly with a fake laugh. "HA-HA! Very funny and original. More short jokes from the imbecile."

Uncle Al whispered in my ear, "Ain't that the little piece of America overseas?"

I put my hand up to prevent Henry and Sabrina from reading my lips as I spoke softly into Uncle Al's ear. "Naw, that's an embassy Unc. He called you an imbecile, which I believe is disrespectful. Again, I'm not a hundred percent sure my damn self, but I *think* you're supposed to be mad right now."

Uncle Al reached to grab my shoulder while speaking directly in my ear. "Man, thanks Nephew. I appreciate that." Then he turned to Henry, yelling, "HOW DARE YOU CALL ME AN EMBASSY!"

I nudged his elbow and mumbled, "Imbecile Unc. Imbecile."

Henry and Sabrina appeared confused as Uncle Al corrected himself. "Yeah! How dare you call me an imbecile!"

Henry grunted with his fists balled as he began to walk toward Uncle Al. Sabrina rapidly grabbed Henry from behind, telling him to ignore Uncle Al because he wasn't worth his time. Henry was still breathing hard when Sabrina asked him to take the elevator down to the gift shop and buy some flowers for Nancy. All of a sudden, the officer who had given us a ride over walked up, prompting Uncle Al to leave with him. As the two were headed out, I walked Henry to the elevator nearby because I knew he would need some help reaching the buttons.

I was almost back in front of Nancy's hospital room door when Tiffany ran out and into my arms again. This time it was with tears of joy and a smile. "My mom is going to make it!"

I kissed and squeezed her during our brief moment of celebration before the doctor and nurse walked out to address us. "She did suffer a concussion. However, she was able to regain consciousness, and we believe she is doing just fine. We will be back in an hour or so to run some necessary tests, but you all can rest assured that she will be back to her normal self at home in no time. Merry Christmas."

The doctor and nurse had started to walk away when Sabrina stopped them both with her aggressively raised tone of voice. "So you mean to tell me, some fifty-five-year-old woman can bust her head and be knocked out. Then, within minutes, she's fine?"

The doctor answered, "Exactly ma'am. This is a common misfortune for people of all ages."

Dissatisfied with his answer, Sabrina had one hand on her hip and the other hand pressing against the wall when she pouted. "Em. Well, that's just unheard of to me."

I thought to myself, *Everything is unheard of to your deaf ass.* We all verbally expressed our sincerest gratitude, and even Sabrina gave the doctor a hug before he and the nurse walked away.

When the doctor and nurse had walked far enough down the hallway for Sabrina not to hear them anymore, which wasn't far at all, she cracked the door open far enough to stick her head through. Then, with a smile that stretched clear across her face, Sabrina called us over with a murmur. "Come here. You guys have to see this." Tiffany and I hurried to the door to pop our heads in as well.

Nancy sat up on the narrow hospital bed with a bunch of machines behind her, although none of them were attached to her. Frank had his chair pressed up against the bed as he looked up at Nancy while holding her hand. I could also hear the faint sound of "Love Comes with Christmas" by the Temptations playing on the small radio in the corner. Nancy had a slight smile on her face as she looked at Frank. "Wow Frank, I never thought you would be the one sitting by my bedside."

Frank chuckled a bit before responding, "I know from the way I act, it seems that way, but I still care about you and love you. In fact, I had been waiting for you to wake up, so that I could apologize for how I've been treating you since you moved back in."

Nancy's head snapped back in shock as she questioned, "Really Frank? You want to apologize to *me*?"

To show sincerity, Frank used both his hands to hold her hand. "Yeah I know, but we were married for over thirty years. I've been with you longer than I've been without you, and you still have my heart. There's no money, concussion, or even divorce that can change that. My love for you is unconditional. Unfortunately, this incident had to happen for me to realize that." Frank stood up to wrap his arms around Nancy's shoulders.

Nancy's eyes began to water, with her head resting on his chest. "I love you too Frank, unconditionally. I always have, and I always will. I know I never told you this, but I really appreciate you. Even throughout our bickering, you made sure I was taken care of. I never had to worry about going without. Frank Mitchell, you're the greatest Christmas gift I've ever had."

While Frank was in the middle of telling Nancy that she was his greatest Christmas gift as well, Tiffany shoved me to the side. Then she took off running to stick her head in the trash can down the hallway. After chasing her down, I stood over top of Tiffany and rubbed her back while she vomited. I sympathized, "It's OK. I know it has to be hard seeing your mom in a hospital bed."

Tiffany stood up to look me in the eye with one hand placed on her stomach. "That's not why Stu. I'm throwing up because I'm pregnant."

My whole upper body leaned backward, like I was trying to dodge a punch. Tiffany continued, "I found out a couple of days ago. I wanted to tell you today, with it being Christmas and all. I just couldn't seem to find the right time. I'm sorry you had to find out this way."

I took a step back, then waved my hand as I shook my head. "No, no, it's OK. It's OK."

When Tiffany saw my reaction, she asked, "What's wrong Stu? I thought you would be excited about it."

The reason I'd stepped back had nothing to do with the pregnancy. It was her post vomit breath. Every time she talked, I thought I was standing in a Porta Potty. I couldn't tell her that though, so I said, "No, I am excited. I'm just taking it all in."

Tiffany smiled. "Oh OK. I can't wait to see how you are with a newborn."

I thought to myself, *I couldn't be happier to be a dad in nine months, but I won't live to see this newborn if you keep talking.* Her last comment had more stank on it than a fish cooler. So I reached down in my pocket and gave Tiffany my last two sticks of chewing gum. She looked up at me, questioning, "Are you sure about this Stu? You don't want to keep one of these sticks for yourself?"

I looked her in the eye and said, "Tiffany, I've never been more sure about something in my life."

———

A little over a month had passed since that unforgettable Christmas, and I found myself back in Santa Monica, California. Much like how Tiffany felt after her first weekend with my family, I'd had a good time and grew to love her family as my own. I just didn't want to do it again.

Nevertheless, here I was, walking into this contemporary-style church to witness these two get remarried in holy matrimony. Teresa stood outside in front of the double entry doors, at the top of the cement steps. Already not wanting to be there, I took a deep breath and blew out hard to prepare myself for whatever drama Teresa might bring my way. Tiffany, who was holding my hand, squeezed it tighter and said in a soft tone, "Stu, just ignore her. We're walking straight to our seats."

Tiffany wore a white paternity dress with beige and brown accents. She was developing beautifully in her pregnancy with her barely visible baby bump. Her skin even had that glow that I always hear mothers speak of.

As we reached the top of the stairs, Teresa approached us, speaking humbly. "Hey Sis. Hey Stuart. I'm glad you all were able to make it out to their wedding. I wanted to tell you both that I thought long and hard about what you all said to me at Christmas dinner, and I want to apologize. I should've never disrespected either one of you, or your marriage."

Tiffany and I looked at each other with big eyes, in shock. After Tiffany accepted Teresa's apology, I said, "Thank you, that means a lot to me to hear you say that. I'm sorry too. I feel like I could've handled that situation in a more mature manner. For the record, I respect the fact that you have your own hair salon. I know it takes a lot of hard work and dedication, regardless of its location. Maybe before we fly back to Maryland, you could do Tiffany's hair." Tiffany dropped her head and walked in the church. As I chased after her, I turned around to say, "Oh, and I'm not trying to play matchmaker or anything, but you know my brother Shane has been asking about you for a while now."

Teresa said with a grin, "Yeah, I saw he requested me as a friend on Facebook. I don't know, we'll see what happens." I nodded and continued into the church.

Now standing in the lobby, I saw another set of double doors in front of me, which led to the sanctuary, and a white door off to the left with a sheet of paper taped to it that read, "Goons Dressing Rum." The simple fact that it was misspelled gave me an idea of the type of wedding I was in for. Since Tiffany had already gone in the sanctuary without me, I decided to go say hi and give early con-gratulations. After I knocked, the door opened, and all I saw were gator boots, cufflinks, and perfectly tailored tuxedos. Impressed, all I could say was, "Got dang! As clean as you are, I'm a have to call you Mr. Mitchell today." We all laughed as I said congratulations and met all the groomsmen.

Soon after, he sat down and opened a container full of Viagra. I warned, "Whoa, don't do that."

He took the pill, then replied, "See, that's your problem Stuart. You always worried. These pills take forty-five minutes to take hold. By that time, we'll be in the limo, so I can get mine on the way to the reception."

I explained, "I've never seen a black wedding start on time. We will see though, because the countdown is on now." I said my good-byes, then went and took my seat in the sanctuary next to Tiffany.

As I expected, the wedding started late. Mr. Mitchell came down the aisle so hard, when he turned to face his bride, they looked like the letter *H*. The reverend began, "We are gathered today for the union of Sister Barbara Patterson and Deacon George Mitchell."

Happily married and the father of two children, Shelton Johnson is a sports fanatic. A former collegiate athlete, Johnson now enjoys coaching, fishing, grilling, and, of course, writing. Johnson attempts to write accessible and enjoyable stories that keep his readers laughing out loud. You can follow him on Twitter @TheWriterSJ for the latest updates to his future projects.

www.ingramcontent.com/pod-product-compliance
Lightning Source LLC
Chambersburg PA
CBHW021116130626
46554CB00002B/727